CW01080203

Precious

Child

ELISABETH C. THOMPSON

ATLANTIS PUBLICATIONS

© Elisabeth C. Thompson 2010
Precious Child

ISBN : 978-0-9556971-3-5

Published by
Atlantis Publications
11, Guildford Place
Chichester
West Sussex
PO19 5DU

A CIP catalogue record of this book
can be obtained from the British Library.

Designed & produced by Michael Walsh at
THE BETTER BOOK COMPANY
5 Lime Close, Chichester, West Sussex PO19 6SW

www.thebetterbookcompany.com

and printed by
IMPRINTDIGITAL
Seychelles Farm, Upton Pyne,
Exeter EX5 5HY

www.imprintdigital.net

For Florence, George and Lily, without whom this book would never have been written and for my godmother, Dorothy, for being there.

There'll be new dreams,
maybe better dreams and plenty

Joni Mitchell

1

"Some people say evolution has programmed us for happiness. Looking around the church today I can see smiles down every aisle. That's proof enough for me."

Mike Chisholm's mind wandered as Fr. Philip continued with his address. "This may not be a wedding in the strict sense of the word, but it is a blessing, so let's all wish Ian and Pippa joy as they set off on their matrimonial journey, the first step of which they took yesterday up in Hardale." His hands appeared from beneath his surplice and he clapped loudly and deliberately which motivated the congregation to follow his lead.

Mike's hands stayed firmly attached to his knees. He stared at the large wooden crucifix in the sanctuary. It was a blessing, of that there could be no doubt, but two ceremonies in two days? Most people would have been satisfied with one. He had not voiced any criticism of his brother's choice. He was relieved to see him happy. Pippa had turned things round for him. She had come into his life at just the right moment and he reckoned their marriage was meant to be. He was confident that for them, *till death us do part*, would mean exactly that, but two ceremonies? Overkill.

The applause died down and Fr. Philip continued with his homily. Mike was fidgeting in his seat, the trousers of his smart blue suit slipping on the mahogany pew, polished to a deep shine over the years by countless other Sunday best suits. He was thinking of a conversation he'd had with his brother a few weeks before.

They had been going over events leading up to the wedding and in particular that rainy morning the previous February when Ian and Pippa had first met. She had knocked on the door of twenty-seven Blain Gardens to value some of their mother's old furniture which was destined for the auction rooms and Ian had recognised her as being a contemporary of his at North Street Primary School. He said he knew, almost from the first moment, that she was the one.

Mike was not a believer in the concept of love at first sight, but he accepted his brother felt that way. He was a practical man with no more romance in him than a flea. Ian was a romantic, a dreamer; never happier than when he had his head in a book. The only books Mike read were health and safety manuals or the most up to date version of the Building Regulations.

Fr. Philip cracked a joke which elicited some quiet laughter. It was wasted on Mike. For the moment, he was concentrating on the reception. It was to be held in a marquee which had materialised in his back garden over the past few days, erupting from the soil like some giant alien mushroom. He hoped it would now be bustling with caterers laying tables and polishing glasses. He wanted to be back at Migay Lodge to check that everything was going according to plan.

His mind could not settle and the marquee was soon put to one side as it moved on to his mother. Never having been a fan of her *old tat*, as he had thought of it, he had been surprised at the success of the sale which had also included some of her china. He had now had the time to research Clarice Cliff and had come to the conclusion that she must have known what she was doing. He had more respect for her skill at bargain hunting.

He remembered other things about her. He knew she had yearned to see Ian settled. It was sad that she had passed away before she'd had time to meet Pippa. She would have liked her. She would have enjoyed this service. Church and her faith had been important to her.

He called to mind his days at Sunday school. The summer parties, hosted by the vicar's wife in the vicarage gardens; the treasure hunts, delicious teas and sense of excitement he had felt at going home time when he was allowed to plunge his five-year-old fingers into the soft warm sawdust of the lucky dip barrel, knowing he would find a prize in there. The triumph on pulling out a parcel; the pleasure at guessing what the tantalising shape might be and then the delight of finding a new toy.

His eyes darkened as he thought of the annual Harvest Festival celebrations. Each year, come September, his mother would insist on both boys preparing a basket of fruit to present at the altar. Mike had harboured a secret desire to offer up a loaf of bread fashioned into a sheaf of wheat instead, but he had never told his mother. He knew she would have said, "No". To her mind a basket of fruit was the way to go and a basket of fruit it had always been. Appealing to his father would have been useless. Norman Chisholm had deferred to his wife in church matters.

It was not only the fancy loaf that had eluded him. The annual Christmas nativity plays had been cast without him in the plum role of Joseph he had coveted so much and that omission still rankled.

His eyes skimmed the stained glass windows with their familiar portrayal of passages from the Bible. The bright sunlight made their colours unbearably beautiful; vivid reds and blues shot through with emerald and gold.

The story of Samson was one of his favourites. With a gentle finger he traced the contours of his nose and pictured himself as a small boy, trying to get his arms around the stone pillars supporting the church roof and grazing it in the process.

His eyes moved higher. He noticed a patch of damp on the east wall where one of the arched windows abutted the roof. He would mention it to Fr. Philip. Putting that to rights would be a nice little job for Chisholm Construction.

Chisholm Construction. He repeated the words slowly to himself under his breath. The company was his baby. He had nurtured it, worked hard to build it up into the profitable concern it now was. Who knows how many back-breaking hours he had put in to achieve its success, how many bricks he had laid. How many cold winter's mornings had seen him stepping through muddy building sites, all alone, icy winds numbing his fingers and blasting his face, just to get a job done on time. He shivered at the thought of it. These days he paid others to do that for him.

His ambition was to become the linchpin of a thriving family firm and in the last few weeks this looked closer to being realised with his brother agreeing to work with him on a new housing development. He could not wait for his two girls to get married and present him with a brace of grandsons to carry on the business. Or even for Ian and Pippa to produce a son to take over the reins. Yes, he thought to himself, perhaps that would be a better idea. Another young Chisholm to carry on the family name. *Chisholm Construction & Nephew.* It had a good ring to it.

"Mike. Stand up," his wife hissed. She pulled gently on his arm and Mike, torn away from his imaginings, got to his feet a little giddily. He grabbed the pew in front to steady himself and realised that the organ was playing again and service sheets were rustling all around him, heralding the final hymn.

2

Outside the church, a glorious summer afternoon awaited the invited guests. The sun was blazing down from a cloudless sky of cerulean blue. It warmed the hips and trusses of the old church and eased its well-worn bricks, while at the same time bringing everything in the Cathedral town of Linchester into sharp focus and encouraging the small white flowers on the privet hedges surrounding the church, to give off their heady perfume.

Being July, the town's population had almost doubled in size. Flurries of holidaymakers had descended on Linchester. They had discovered and appreciated its historic pedigree and sheltered picturesque position under the generous shoulders of the South Downs, not too far from the coast.

Passers-by licking fast-melting ice creams turned their heads to gaze on the bridal procession emerging from the open doors of St. Jude's. It was a fine example of a red brick Victorian church and worthy of note in its own right. They paused a while, to watch the photographer. He was waiting for the assembled throng, surrounded by his attendant paraphernalia and a nervous assistant who was scurrying this way and that, preparing suitable tableaux for his employer to capture for Pippa's luxury album. The price he had charged for his services that afternoon was almost as outrageous as his flamboyant style of dress, but she had been taken with his textured prints and misty, romantic shots and had ignored the expense. The onlookers smiled knowingly at each other, calling to mind other weddings at other times in other places and then, one by one, they sauntered off to re-connect with their own lives.

"Have you got the rose petals, Marge?" asked Susie, Mike's youngest. She was, like her mother, slim and blonde and, like her father, not backward in coming forward. She loved to use this special name for her mother whenever he was within earshot. It was guaranteed to annoy him, a definite bonus in her eyes. Susie loved to tease, another characteristic she shared with her father. It made family life at Migay Lodge interesting, to say the least. Mike's unwillingness to compromise and Susie's high spirits often led to spats between the two of them. It was fortunate Gaynor was a patient woman and an expert at soothing damaged egos. She told her friends that life was never dull when Susie was home from university.

She produced a bulky paper bag from her brown Birkin-style handbag and handed it over to her daughter. "Here. I bought two boxes so that you and Jane could spread them around a bit."

Ivy Ellison had been watching this exchange. She moved slowly towards Susie, massaging her left hip as she walked. "Is that confetti?" she said. "I forgot to bring mine."

Gaynor smiled at their old friend. "They're rose petals, Ivy. But you're more than welcome to some."

Susie opened one of the boxes and handed over a generous pink handful. "Is that enough? There's loads in the box."

"Yes, that's plenty, dear. Thanks very much. I'll just put them in here so they don't blow away."

Ivy stuffed the petals into the deep pockets of her tight-fitting jacket. Worn over a bright, floral dress, it was grass green with a generous collar, three-quarter length sleeves and oversized mother-of-pearl buttons redolent of the 1950s. Her clothes were always colourful, if not entirely in keeping with modern tastes. Due to the generosity of her late husband, her wardrobe had been well stocked with clothes over the years and she saw no reason to buy anything new now, just for the sake of it, while she could still fasten the buttons and zips on her current stash.

Susie was standing on tiptoes, craning her neck over the myriad of exotic headgear in search of her sister. "Can you see Jane anywhere? I hope these are biodegradable."

"Of course they are. I checked. And no, I haven't seen Jane."

"I've seen her," said a voice from beneath one of the most eye-catching hats present. Fuchsia pink with a tall crown and profusion of nodding ostrich feathers, it belonged to Isobel Flynn. "She's over by the gate talking to Beth from Pippa's office. See? Beth's wearing a pale blue cap."

"Cheers, Isobel." Susie teetered off towards the gate in her blue patent sling backs, her dress rustling and shimmering with iridescent hues as the sunlight caught the teal taffeta when she moved.

Gaynor turned away from watching her daughter's precarious progress and smiled at her companions. "I don't think you know Edith Gill, do you Ivy? She's Isobel's mother and, of course, Pippa's grandmother. She's travelled all the way down from Cumbria to be here today. Edith, Ivy Ellison."

Ivy sheltered from the hot sun under her broad-brimmed red straw hat and nodded welcomingly at Edith. "Pleased to meet you. I've known Ian since he was a little boy. They make a lovely couple don't they?"

"They certainly do," Edith said in her pleasant Cumbrian lilt. "Are you the Ivy who lives next door to them?"

Ivy nodded vigorously. "That's right." Her thick white waves bounced up and down beneath the hat, making it bob about like a buoy on the swell. She put up a hand to steady it.

"Weren't you in hospital a little while back? I think Pippa was quite worried about you."

"Bless her. Yes, I was. It was my chest. Double Pneumonia. I nearly coughed myself silly." Having a captive audience, Ivy started on a thorough résumé of her recent stay at St. Peter's.

Gaynor and Isobel exchanged smiles. Gaynor was particularly pleased that the two old ladies were chatting away happily as she had seated them together at the top table. It was clear they would have plenty to talk about.

Ian and Pippa, meanwhile, were in the middle of a thorough photo-shoot. The photographer's assistant was rounding up the guests for a shot of everybody, including their border terrier, Millie. She was enjoying all the attention. She sat quietly, accepting the guests' adulation, the special silver collar she had worn at the wedding the previous day sparkling in the sun as they bent down to stroke her head and marvel at how well-behaved she had been in church.

"Nearly finished," called the photographer. "After this one, you can all throw your confetti."

Pippa giggled and then turned to whisper into Ian's ear, "I hope no-one's brought rice. I don't fancy a black eye."

"We'll make a run for the car if they have."

"Not in these shoes," she said. She looked down at her crystal-encrusted high heels. The beads of glass glinting there were a perfect match to the ones painstakingly sewn all over the bodice of her ivory satin dress and set in the tiara, which flashed and sparkled in her auburn hair. "What car?" she asked all of a sudden, only just picking up on his last comment, "We didn't order a car to take us to Mike's house."

"You might not have done," Ian said. He smiled at her. "Wait and see."

He hoped the hire company was not going to let him down. He deliberately ignored her intrigued, "What's going on?" and when the photographer was finally satisfied with his efforts and had released them to head off for the reception, he grabbed her hand and guided her towards the gate, stopping briefly to chat to guests on the way.

The first one waiting to offer congratulations was their old teacher, Jacinta Scott. She was, as ever, dressed with impeccable taste. She had chosen to wear a silk suit in eau de Nil and, having no time for hats, had placed a small velvet bow on the back of her head beneath her trademark bun, which sat like a pompom on the top of her head.

"Well done, you two. You look lovely, Pippa," she said, brown eyes smiling from behind rimless glasses.

"Thank you. I'm so pleased you came," Pippa said.

Ian smiled at Miss Scott and nodded in agreement. "Have you got transport to the reception?"

"Yes, thank you. Isobel and Adrian are giving me a lift."

"See you there, then."

"Yes. See you later."

They moved on. Ian's eyes darted up and down the road as they accepted more well-meaning compliments from friends and family. He left Pippa to make the necessary responses. He was willing the car to appear. At last his silent prayers were answered by the unmistakable rumble of a V8 engine. Pippa heard it, too. She stopped chatting to look down the road with him, her face fast becoming a picture of astonishment as a bright red, low-slung, open-top sports car drew up alongside the church and stopped.

Ian let go of her hand and walked across to the car. The driver emerged, handed the keys over to him and after a brief conversation he walked off, leaving Ian to rejoin his stunned bride. "Your carriage awaits, my lady," he said with a low bow, placing the keys in her hand.

"Am I supposed to *drive* that?" she asked, her green eyes displaying her disbelief.

He was grinning now. "That's the general idea."

Pippa giggled her endearing giggle and then remembered her promise to Beth. She glanced around trying to locate her friend in the crowd. The sea of faces almost defeated her until she caught a glimpse of Beth's jaunty blue cap and aimed her bouquet in that general direction. It sailed through the air and hit its mark with impressive accuracy. She picked up her skirt and amid a whirlwind of rose petals and startled exclamations, she stepped over the hot exhaust pipe, kicked off her shoes and eased herself into the driving seat of the sports car.

Mike and Gaynor were just getting into their four by four in the church car park when they became aware of all the excitement on the pavement outside.

"What's all that about?" Mike asked. He pulled his sunglasses down from the top of his head and peered through the windscreen, trying to get a clear view of the road, but the flagpole and privet hedges obscured his field of vision.

Gaynor could see everything from her side of the car. "It looks like Ian and Pippa are going to drive off in a red sports car. Did you know anything about this?"

"No. Well, I knew Ian had booked some sort of a car to take them to the reception, but I didn't think any further than that," Mike said. "I suppose I presumed it would be a taxi…" He stopped for a minute, opened the car door and, holding on to the roof with one hand whilst balancing his feet on the sill, he strained his body to get a better look at things. He whistled in admiration. "… not an AC Cobra."

Pippa slotted the keys into the ignition and waited for Ian to join her. She removed her tiara, dropping it nonchalantly onto his knees the minute he sat down. "Here goes, then. Don't shout if I clash the gears." Her foot came off the brake and on to the accelerator. She released the clutch and the car roared off down the road, drowning out the cheers from the assembled crowd.

Mike slid back into his car. "We'll see about that," he said as he revved up the four by four and gave chase.

3

Pippa's face ached, but not in a bad way. She had smiled at so many people and kissed so many cheeks that she felt quite weary. She wondered how the Queen managed, having to greet people in a similar fashion day after day, week after week.

A small person in a tight black dress which seemed to be moulded to her body, appeared beside them. She was carrying a tray of drinks and nibbles. Her brown hair was lacquered up into wings on either side of her face and her slightly prominent teeth, which crouched on her bottom lip as if under starter's orders, together with her eyebrows which were finely drawn a little too high on her forehead, had left her in a permanent state of astonishment. "Would you like a Buck's Fizz?" she asked. "A canapé, perhaps?"

"Ooh, yes please," Pippa said, helping herself to both. "Thanks. The marquee's turned out well, hasn't it?"

"I'm glad you like it, Mrs. Chisholm. My team worked hard on it. Congratulations, by the way." Pippa thanked her again and then watched as she waited just long enough for Ian to take a glass from her tray, before moving on to offer refreshments elsewhere.

"Who was that?" he asked.

"Carolyn," Pippa said. "Mike had dragged you off somewhere when Gaynor introduced me. She runs this catering company very efficiently, despite her size."

"I can see that. I'm impressed."

"So you should be." Pippa gave his arm a squeeze. "She's done well. Don't you think it looks good?"

"It's amazing."

He gazed around the marquee, which was decorated with the blue and cream theme Pippa had requested. There were several round tables covered in cream damask cloths. A single white rose in a slender blue vase marked the centre of each one. Next to the name cards was a disposable camera, plus as a favour for each guest, a cellophane-wrapped trio of Belgian chocolates. The heavy silver cutlery, chosen for its simple modern elegance, gleamed solidly from the place settings laid at regular intervals round the edge of the tables, calling to mind the numerals on the face of a clock.

A wide blue sash was looped along the length of the top table. It was pinned at either end to the crease-free cloth which covered not only the top of the table but also fell down over its sides, camouflaging the legs and arriving at the floor in generous creamy folds. The finishing touch was a magnificent spray of cornflowers and white roses fixed at the central point by trailing blue and cream ribbons.

His eyes floated upwards to swing with the clutches of blue and cream helium balloons which swayed at random above and beside the tables. Mike's sole input to the dressing of the marquee had been the supply of engineering bricks, now camouflaged in sheet upon sheet of blue tissue paper tweaked into spiralling peaks, to which these balloons were tethered.

"She's certainly transformed this marquee," he said. "The last time I was in here, it looked like a scouts' mess tent. Now it has the distinct air of a palace about it."

Pippa giggled. "That's funny. Talking of palaces, I was just thinking about the Queen. Do you think we're psychic now we're married?"

"Oh, I don't know if I'll ever be able to read your mind, SweetP, but it's a nice thought. Have we spoken to everyone, now?"

"We must have. We've been standing here for ages."

Ian glanced across at his father's cousin, who seemed to be sharing a joke with Miss Scott. "Dave looks good, doesn't he? Retirement seems to suit him. It's a shame Jim couldn't come."

"You didn't expect him to give up three weeks in New Zealand, did you?"

"No, of course not. He's been planning that trip for months. Dave said he was going to ring him in the week. Tell him how all this went off."

"He did send us a card."

"Yes, he did and he managed the stag night. They're very alike, those two. Always doing something. I can't believe Dave packs so much into his life at his age. Cycling, bird watching, football."

"I know. How old is he?"

"Seventy at the end of the year. Both he and Mike are on the management committee of Linchester Wanderers now. I thought Mike was bad enough, but Dave seems to be even more hard core where the football is concerned. I think he's taken *use it or lose it* to heart."

Pippa giggled. "I didn't meet his wife. Is she here?"

"We don't mention her," Ian said. "They were divorced years ago. Pam left him to bring up Jim on his own."

"Oh. That's sad. It must have been hard for him. I've never actually met your cousin, you know ...."

Ian interrupted her. "Erm, second cousin," he said with a smile. "Mike and I don't have any proper cousins."

"... alright. If it makes you happy, *second* cousin. Garth and Mike were the only ones with you when you came back after your stag night. I didn't see Jim." Pippa gave him a meaningful glance. She was thinking back to that particular evening and remembering how Mike had returned to the house mumbling incoherently and needing assistance to lift him from the hall floor where he had settled down, his back against the wall, smiling foolishly to himself.

Ian grinned. He knew precisely what she was thinking. "Well, he's more than made up for all that now. He's certainly gone the extra mile this time. The marquee is fantastic."

Pippa nodded in agreement. "It was very kind of him to loan us his back garden and to organise the marquee and *extremely* generous of him to foot the bill ... but you and I both know who did most of the hard work." She stared straight across at her new sister-in-law who had her back turned to them as she chatted with some of the other guests. "I'm glad that thunderstorm put paid to our original plans. This is a much better venue than the barn over at Brierley."

"Really?"

"Oh yes. Don't you think so? I hope we sit down to eat soon. I'm beginning to feel a bit light-headed."

"We should have had some lunch. It can't be long now, surely." Getting ready for the service had been such a rush that they had both skipped lunch. It did not help that hints of the food being prepared for the wedding breakfast were beginning to waft into the marquee. Whiffs of smoked salmon, Boeuf Bourguignon and Crème Brulée were curling their way into every crevice. "Let's mingle while we're waiting. It might take our minds off food."

"Ok." Pippa said, although she thought that unlikely the way her stomach was grumbling at her. As she sipped at her drink and nibbled her last remaining square of pâté-encrusted toast, they tried to agree on who should be first for the mingling. Before they had time to reach a consensus, they were joined by Tim. "Where on earth did you find that car?"

"I thought you'd like it," Ian said. "On the internet, of course. Where else?"

"Ah. The World Wide Web. I should have known. Nice exit. A pity it had to go back. I would have loved to have had a go myself; although I'm more of a biker. What I really came to ask you is where we should set up. The rest of the band has arrived now."

"Not sure. Pippa?"

They turned round to scan the marquee and noticed Susie heading their way. "Hi, Tim," she said, ignoring the bride and groom. "Mum says will you have room in that corner opposite the top table?"

Pippa smiled at her brother. "Well, there's your answer, Tim. Gaynor's in charge."

He looked at the space mentioned. "I think that'll do as long as there's a nearby socket for our amps."

"Dad will know," Susie declared confidently. "Come on." She took hold of Tim's arm and dragged him off to find Mike.

Carolyn reappeared at Ian's shoulder. "Could you take your seats now please?"

"We're on our way," he said, cupping Pippa's elbow in his hand and gently urging her forward. They headed for the top table, which was the cue for all the other guests to find their places.

Alice Forbes was already sitting down, because with only one month to go, she had reached the stage in her pregnancy where standing for any length of time was rather a trial. Pippa decided to have a quick word with her.

As they got closer to her table, she noticed a glowing on her friend's forehead. "Hang on Ian," she said. "Are you alright, Alice? You look a bit hot."

"I am a bit hot." Alice wiped a tissue above her eyebrows leaving her carefully arranged fringe slightly askew.

"It is quite warm, today," Ian said.

Alice wafted her order of service round her head. "Yes. Perfect weather for a wedding."

"Better day than we had," Simon said.

"I remember," Pippa said. "It poured all day. It was still a lovely wedding, though."

"Shame about the photographs," he said.

Alice laughed. "They weren't that bad. Well, they would have been better if the photographer's flash gun hadn't gone all wrong. He was expecting to take most of them outside." She flinched and patted her burgeoning stomach. "Ouch. This little one seems to be auditioning for the Olympic gymnastics' team," she said. "Good job you decided not to ask me to be your bridesmaid, Pippa. I'm uncomfortable standing, I'm uncomfortable sitting for too long and my back aches practically the whole time. I bet you're sorry you asked me how I was feeling, now. It's not for much longer, though, is it? I'll be glad when it's all over." She sighed and took another sip from her tall glass of iced water.

Simon seemed alarmed. "Hold it right there," he said. "I haven't finished painting the baby's bedroom, yet. We don't want things to happen for a couple of weeks at least."

"Oh, all right. I'll hold on until then, shall I?" she said, a slight edge to her voice.

Pippa gave her a sympathetic smile. "I don't think you'll have much say in the matter. Don't babies have a habit of suiting themselves? I can't wait to see what it is, though. Have you decided on names?"

"I have, but Simon doesn't agree. Do you, hun?"

"I like your choice of girls' names," Simon said. "It's some of the boys' names I think are a bit iffy. Would you like your son to be called *Maximilian*, Pippa?"

Pippa caught Ian's eye and they exchanged amused glances. "I'm not getting involved," she said.

Alice was not happy. "My husband's got no taste. I don't know what the problem is. There's absolutely nothing wrong with *Max* as a name. We've got plenty of time to decide anyway. You never know. I might come up with something else."

"That sounds ominous," Simon said.

"She can't possibly choose anything worse than Jeremiah, which is what my Mum and Dad picked for Mike's middle name."

Alice adopted a serious expression. "Ah … that's an idea. Jeremiah Forbes …"

Simon shook his head. "No," he said firmly.

Before any more suggestions could be made, Ian and Pippa's pint-sized nemesis materialised in front of them. The astonishment had morphed into fierce. "We're ready to serve the first course, if you could take your seats *now* please," she said standing her ground, arms folded, brooking no argument.

"Yes, right. Sorry," Ian said, hastily. "We're on our way. Come on, SweetP."

4

Mike had planned his speech meticulously. As best man, he knew that according to etiquette, he should really speak last but Ian and Adrian had both agreed he should start the speech-making, seeing as the reception was being held at Migay Lodge.

As soon as the coffee had been served, he stood up and cleared his throat. "Well, some of you guys out there might think you're something special," he began, "But I have it on very good authority that I am the *best* man." This set the light-hearted tone for the rest of his speech. He spoke with surprising eloquence and started by paying tribute to his parents followed by a short history of his and Ian's childhood and then Ian's civil engineering career.

"Now to the present. As you know, Ian's having a career break at the moment. He assures me his globe-trotting days are over and, reading between the lines, I can't help thinking this has a lot to do with Pippa. The day they met was a very lucky one for him. She managed to do something we had all failed to do. She made him smile again." He stopped and waited for the spontaneous clapping to subside. "We all love her. She's one of us, now." He turned to face her and raised his glass. "Thanks, we owe you one, Pippa. I just want to add that you two won't go far wrong if you're as happy as Gaye and I have been over the last, nearly twenty-five, years. Finally, it's my duty to propose a toast to the bridesmaids." He raised his glass again. "To my daughters, Jane and Susie, or as I like to call them, the two lovely ladies in waiting ... Jane and Susie."

Ian felt he had got off rather lightly. He had braced himself for a long list of humiliating incidents from his brother and was relieved that Mike had only mentioned one discomfiting moment from their childhood. That had been more of an embarrassment for Mike than for him. It was all to do with a cricket ball and a broken window. Their father had seen Mike retrieving his ball after the sound of shattering glass had sent him rushing outside. Despite protestations of his innocence, Mike had been the one held to account until Ian's conscience had finally forced him to admit that it had been his shot that had done the damage. They had both had their pocket money stopped for several weeks to help pay for the replacement glass. Their father had decided that Mike, as instigator of the game, was partly to blame. He should have chosen a more sensible place to play. He was, after all, six years older than his brother.

Next, it was Adrian's turn. He gave his glasses a quick polish and smoothed down his tie before he stood up. "I don't intend to speak for too long," he said, which elicited the anticipated uproarious applause and a few cat calls. He had to wait for all the noise to die down before he could carry on. "Before I say anything else, I'd like to thank Mike and Gaynor for allowing us to invade their garden and for setting up this splendid marquee for us all to enjoy." He looked across to where Mike and Gaynor were sitting and nodded his thanks.

There was a short delay for more applause and then he started again. "My daughter, Pippa, has always known her own mind. She is, in my view, a very sensible girl. I knew I was right about that when she agreed to marry Ian. Isobel and I are both proud to have him as our son-in-law. I think they're well suited and I'm sure they will be very happy together. Well that's about it. So, ladies and gentlemen, would you please raise your glasses to my beautiful daughter, Pippa and her bridegroom, Ian."

Adrian sat down as the last 'Ian and Pippa' faded away and then it was Ian's turn. Pippa squeezed his hand in encouragement. He had not told her word for word what he was planning to say, but she knew he had been nervous about standing up and speaking in front of so many people.

"My speech is also going to be very short," he said with a disarming smile. "Firstly I have a few people to thank, starting with all of you for coming here today and for your generous gifts. Thanks, everyone. Then I'd like to thank my brother Mike and his wife, Gaynor, for all the effort they have put in to making our reception so perfect, but extra special thanks must go to Gaynor, because all of this was her idea." He indicated that he meant the marquee and its entire contents with a wide sweep of his arms.

"As most of you know, our first plan was to have the reception in a barn over at Brierley, but when a thunderstorm put paid to that, Gaynor came up with this idea and Pippa and I are unbelievably grateful to her for having saved the day." He turned to face Gaynor and started to clap, which encouraged the same response from everyone else and made Gaynor shake her head and blush with embarrassment.

"Another important thank you goes to our lovely bridesmaids, Jane and Susie. Thanks both of you." He raised his glass to his nieces, who both raised theirs back. "And also to Adrian and Isobel for producing such a beautiful daughter. My biggest thank you, though, must go to my wife, Pippa." He hesitated for a moment while there was even more applause and a few raucous cheers. "Who has made me happy beyond my wildest dreams. So, please raise your glasses to my wonderful wife, Pippa." Now it was Pippa's turn to go pink, but from pleasure this time and not embarrassment like Gaynor.

A few seats along from Ian, Isobel, Ivy and Edith sat smiling and nodding their approval while Mike raised his glass, took a sip of the champagne and then stood up and clapped more enthusiastically than anyone else in the marquee until Gaynor pulled him back down to whisper something in his ear. He nodded and stood up again, banging the back of his spoon on the table as he did so. "Let's have a bit of hush," he shouted above the general hubbub. He waited for the chattering to die away. "When the tables have been cleared, we're going to be entertained by Pippa's brother with the band, *Nimbus*. Enjoy the music and feel free to get up and dance if you want to."

He sat back down again, only to have to stand up once more, a few minutes later, having been prompted by Gaynor to mention the cake cutting and to read out some greetings cards that had arrived at the last minute.

In the lull that followed Mike's announcements, Ian and Pippa managed a quiet moment together as they surveyed the room and their assembled guests.

"Loved the speech," Pippa said.

"It was a bit nerve-wracking, but I think I did all right. Garth and Chrissie seem to be getting on well with Alice and Simon."

"They do. And don't their twins look sweet in their little white shirts and tartan bow-ties?"

"Yes. I'm surprised they've been so quiet, actually. They're usually such a lively pair. I think they've been at the chocolates." Ian had noticed tell-tale brown smears on the two little round faces. "I'm going to have a word with Tim before the band starts up. Is that alright, wife?"

"Yes, go on. I'd like a chat with Mum anyway. We haven't had a chance to catch up all day."

Isobel was pleased to have Pippa all to herself for a while. "Where are you two going for your honeymoon," she asked as they sat talking together across Ian's empty chair.

Pippa shrugged her shoulders. "No idea. I asked Ian to surprise me and he hasn't said a word about it since. All I know is that after the reception we're driving over to Midhurst to spend the night at the Spread Eagle Hotel. It's where Ivy and Sid had their honeymoon, you know."

"Is it? How romantic, sweetie."

"I love his surprises," Pippa breathed, a faraway look in her eyes as they followed Ian across the marquee. It was taking him longer than anticipated to reach the band, due to the amount of people stopping him to claim their special moment of his time as he passed.

Isobel had noticed Alice standing close by, leaning on the back of a chair as she chatted to James McFarlane and his wife at their table. "How's Alice? Her baby must be due soon. She's quite enormous, isn't she? Is she having twins?"

Pippa giggled. "I'm sure she's not. She told us earlier that the baby's due in a couple of weeks. She can't wait. She's so uncomfortable."

"You can tell Alice from me, that however uncomfortable she is, she'd better make the most of these last few days of peace. Once the baby's here she won't know whether she's on her head or her heels." Then another thought occurred to her. "You're not going to start a family straight away, are you, darling? Do have a couple of years together without children, first. Once they arrive your time won't be your own any more. Or your money, come to think of it. Take it from one who knows."

"Come on, Mum. We haven't even been on our honeymoon, yet. Give us a chance."

Ian, having finished talking with the band, was just about to return to his seat, when he caught sight of Jane emerging from the house through the entrance to the marquee. It reminded him that he wanted to have a word with her. He had a suspicion she might need some moral support when it came to revealing her career plans to her parents and he wanted her to know that she could count on him for that support if necessary. He made his way over to her but James McFarlane got there first.

"Hello, you must be Jane." He held out an introductory hand. "James McFarlane. Pippa works with me at the auction rooms."

"Oh, yes. Nice to meet you, Mr. McFarlane." Jane shook James's outstretched hand.

"She's told me all about the gap year you spent in Africa. I was wondering if we could have a talk about it. My nephew wants to do the same sort of thing."

"What is it you want to know?"

"All the basics, I suppose. Who runs these things, how you get a place on a scheme; how expensive it is and so forth."

Ian hovered behind a bunch of balloons while he waited for them to finish their conversation. He saw Jane jot down a couple of names on the back of one of James's business cards and as soon as he had moved away to pass on the relevant details to his wife, Ian was finally able to seize his chance. He emerged from his hiding place and surprised her. "Hello, Jane. Are you enjoying yourself?"

"Oh. Hi, Uncle Ian, I didn't see you there. Where did you spring from? Yes. It's fantastic. Are you?"

"I am. Very much. It's great to see so many people here."

"Pippa looks cool and I love her Mum's hat," she said.

"It's the same dress as yesterday, you know and the same hat." Ian grinned. "I am a lucky man, though, and I know it. The bridesmaids look *cool*, too." He thought he had better get on with what he had really come to say. "I was wondering when you get your results and what you're planning to do next."

Jane pulled a face. "Don't remind me," she said. "They should come in the post next week. I'm dreading it."

"Why? I'm quite sure you've got nothing to worry about. I know how hard you've worked. So what are your plans for the future?"

She hesitated and then decided she was not ready to tell him the truth. Until her plans had crystallised, she was not going to reveal them to anyone. "I haven't made any firm decisions so far."

This prevarication made her lower her eyes from his gaze. She glanced at his face from under her lashes to see if she could tell what he was thinking. Could he guess her thoughts? Did he know what she had in mind? She reasoned that she would have to tell people soon and it would be sensible to start sharing her aspirations with someone she could claim as an ally. Was that person her uncle? She thought he might be sympathetic but could she take the chance?

Ian, who already had an inkling of the way she was thinking via a circuitous route which involved a hunch his brother-in-law had shared with Pippa, smiled an encouraging smile. "Well, I'm sure you'll make the right decision in the end. If you need some advice, you can always talk to me, or Pippa. Any time," he said and then he had a moment of inspiration. Over Jane's head, he could see Pippa talking with Fr. Philip. "Or you could always speak to Fr. Philip. He's very approachable you know."

Jane looked at her uncle again. This was seriously weird. It seemed as if he *could* read her mind. Otherwise, how could he possibly know she wanted to become a priest? His face gave away no clue whatsoever. He was smiling his shy smile, his startlingly blue eyes calmly returning her gaze. In fact she thought he looked just the way he normally did, except for the sharp suit he was wearing and the white rose in his buttonhole. It was a ridiculous idea. Of course he couldn't know what she wanted to do with her life.

"I'm not ready to discuss my plans with anyone, yet," she replied. "Please don't say anything to Dad about me not knowing what I'm doing. He wants me to go into teaching and I definitely don't want to do that. I really can't stand it when he goes on and on at me."

Ian had often felt the same way. His brother could be like a dog with a bone sometimes and he had played the bone to Mike's worrying too many times not to understand her fears. "Of course I won't. I do think you should have a word with Fr. Philip, though. He could talk you through any problems you might have. Whatever they are. Don't worry about your Dad; I'll put in a good word for you if necessary. I'm sure Pippa will, too." He was not going to probe any further. He hoped she would eventually find the courage to confide in him.

Jane gave him a very hard stare. "It's almost as if you know exactly what I'm thinking." On the spur of the moment she decided to trust him with her secret. "Ok. I'll tell you what I want to do, but you must promise not to breathe a word to Dad ... or anyone else either."

Ian looked solemn. "I promise."

"Well, what I really want to do ..." She stopped abruptly. She had caught sight of her father heading their way.

Ian, who had been silently congratulating himself on finally getting her to reveal her intentions, wondered what had stopped her in her tracks. He turned round to follow her gaze and saw the approach of his brother. His eyes narrowed. He understood. He could not prevent a momentary shadow of irritation from clouding his brow, but it was swiftly replaced with a resigned smile.

The moment had passed. Now there was no chance of Jane admitting what she had in mind. However, he was confident that he had said enough to make her realise he knew what she was contemplating and that he was willing to support her if such support were necessary. If Mike took against it, she would need a flak jacket and ear plugs as well.

"What are you two talking about?" Mike said. "What's up?"

Ian winked at Jane. She gave him the slightest of smiles and then an almost imperceptible nod of her head to let him know that she knew he knew and what a relief that was to her. She did not meet her father's eyes. "Oh, nothing," she said quickly. "I'm just going to check up on Millie," and with that, she disappeared back into the house.

"I'll never understand those girls," Mike said with a sigh. "They did look good in their dresses though, didn't they? I think the whole thing has gone off rather well. When are you leaving?"

Ian was used to his brother's tactless ways. He smiled at him. "You're very keen to get rid of us," he said. "I still have a few people to talk to and I want at least one dance with my wife before we decide to leave. If that's all right with you."

"Of course, of course. Just checking." Mike's next few words were drowned out by the band who had launched in with one of Ian and Pippa's favourite Beatles' numbers. ... *"You say you want a rev-o-oh-lution, we-ell you know, we all want to change the world ..."* He shook his head and walked off.

Ian could not help thinking that Jane would be lucky if her little revolution elicited such a meek response.

5

Adrian sauntered across the marquee to the small dance floor. The fake wood bounced under his tread. He tapped Pippa on her shoulder. The loud music made normal conversation impossible. He addressed her in a robust tone. "I'm taking your gran back to the house."

She was locked in Ian's arms, squeezed between the other couples swaying to and fro in time to the music. As they stopped to listen to her father, it involved some fancy footwork on his part not to trip someone up. "Think she's a bit tired," he finished, wobbling a little on his axis.

Pippa let go of Ian and put her head close to her father's, speaking directly into his ear. "Ok, Dad. We'll come and say goodbye. She's done well to last this long. What do you think of Tim's band?"

"Good. Bit loud," he said and turned on his heel to walk back to his seat.

Ian had been unable to catch their conversation. "What's going on?"

"He's taking Gran home," Pippa said, employing the same method of communication she had used with her father and taking the opportunity to kiss Ian at the same time. "Are you coming to say goodbye to her?"

He nodded and followed her across the marquee.

Fr. Philip saw all this action and smiled affably at Ian and Pippa as they passed by his table. He was sitting on his own, savouring the last few drops of wine in his glass and feeling suitably mellow. He was thinking to himself how friendly the Chisholm and Flynn families were. He was also thinking that the two Chisholm Boys were a credit to their mother.

It occurred to him that it was odd he should think of Mike and Ian in those terms. He and Mike were, after all, almost the same age, but Vera Chisholm's old friends at St. Jude's always referred to them as 'the Chisholm Boys' and that was how they stuck in his mind.

He was relieved and pleased to see Ian looking so happy. He had been worried about him. He supposed it was inevitable that being by far the most sensitive of the two brothers, Ian was hit the hardest by Vera's death. He had spoken with Ivy Ellison on several occasions about what he could do to help and she had advised him to leave Ian to work through his grief in his own way. She was keeping an eye on him; time would do the rest.

It would seem she had been right. Ian's grief was behind him now, thanks to time and, of course, to his charming new wife. Fr. Philip reflected on the fact that the love of a good woman could achieve amazing things. He thought, fondly, of his own wife who was abroad, visiting family. She would be gone for another couple of weeks and he missed her. Never having had children, their relationship was more intense than most and she gave him a great deal of support with parish matters. He rubbed his bearded chin and, looking down, noticed that the glass he was nursing was empty. He reckoned it was time for him to make a move.

The vicar of St. Jude's did not have a monopoly on introspection. From across the dance floor Jane glanced warily at Fr. Philip, summing him up. She had always thought he had the look of a small Italian priest about him and he was certainly an approachable man. Perhaps her uncle was right and she should have a word with him.

She liked his large eyes which were a limpid grey and luminous with understanding and humour. She liked his soft voice and his unassuming manner. She took a deep breath and decided that it was now or never. Fr. Philip was standing up and seemed to be getting ready to leave.

Taking advantage of a lull in the music, she screwed up her courage and moved stiffly over to his table. Nervously, she stood behind his chair, deciding what to say. Addressing the back of his head, she began. "Erm … could I have a quick word with you please?" The words were spoken. She could not take them back now.

Fr. Philip turned round to face her. "Hello, yes of course you can. You're one of Mike's girls aren't you? Sorry, your name escapes me. If my wife was here, she'd know. She has a phenomenal memory. I call her my walking encyclopaedia."

Jane gave him a brittle laugh. "It's Jane."

He smiled. "Of course it is. How can I help you?"

She was having trouble getting the words out. It was as if they had been starched to her tongue. "I'd … just like some career advice, actually …" She hesitated, but knew she had no choice. She had to continue. "I want to go into the ministry."

Fr. Philip raised his eyebrows. "Really? I think this will be more than a *quick* word, then. Perhaps you could come and see me in the parish office some time."

"Yes, perhaps that would be better. I feel a bit exposed here." Her eyes darted about anxiously.

"Right. Now let me see." He was making a brave attempt to check his diary without actually having it with him. "I know. How about Tuesday morning? I think I'm free at about ten o'clock. Is that any good for you?"

"I'm sure I can be there at ten. I'm really grateful. You don't know how much this means to me." Without another word, Jane turned tail and headed straight for the house.

Nimbus started up again and Fr. Philip watched Jane's departing back view, his lips pursed. He ruffled his now sparse dark hair and wondered what he was letting himself in for. This was going to be a tricky one, but who was he to question the mindset of the Almighty? He reckoned that it was just like his Boss to keep him on his toes. He pushed back his chair and went to take his farewells of the bride and groom.

The marquee was slowly emptying. The band were busy taking down microphones and unplugging instruments and the bride and groom were preparing to leave.

"Are you off now, sweetie?"

"Yes. We're all packed up and ready to go," Pippa said. "You will make a fuss of Millie, won't you, Mum? I expect she'll miss us."

The little dog wagged her tail at the mention of her name and seemed to grin at Isobel. She took the lead Pippa was offering her. "Of course we will. Dad's looking forward to walking round all his old haunts with her while you're away. Well, goodbye, darling." Isobel blinked as a tear started to form in the corner of her eye. She gave her daughter an affectionate hug and her sentimental self a silent talking to. At thirty-seven, Pippa was hardly a teenager leaving home for the first time.

"Goodbye, Ian. Look after her, won't you?" Adrian called.

Ian was already outside and heading for the car. "You bet."

"You know he will, Dad." Pippa gave her father one last peck on the cheek, "That's if I *need* looking after." She added one of her inimitable giggles and then a loud, "Goodbye," as she followed Ian out to the car.

"Come on, Mrs. Chisholm," he said. He waited for her to close the car door before he turned the key in the ignition. "Let's go."

"I hope we said goodbye to everyone," Pippa said. "And I hope they all enjoyed themselves."

"I'm certain they did. Well Mike did anyway. He kept coming up to me and saying what a good idea the marquee was ... as if it had all been down to him ... and Mrs.E did. She told me so at least twice. I'm surprised Mike isn't here, waving us off."

"I saw him down at the fishpond earlier. With a torch?"

"That sounds like Mike. He's obsessed with those fish. Probably checking to see whether the noise had disturbed them. As if."

"I think it's quite sweet he cares so much about them. Are you going to tell me where we're going, now?"

"No, not yet. I thought I'd wait until we get to the hotel."

Pippa had to be satisfied with that. However much she continued to wheedle, he would not give her even so much as a clue.

They drove into Midhurst and negotiated the narrow winding streets that led to the Spread Eagle Hotel. Its lights seemed to be beaming a welcome to them. Leaving the car in the hotel car park, they approached the building from the rear and went in through a side door and then along a low-ceilinged passageway. The lights had been dimmed and it was eerily quiet.

They passed a suit of armour standing beside the most enormous cuckoo clock Pippa had ever seen and did not meet a soul on the way to the reception area. It was hardly surprising. It was well after midnight and no longer the weekend; more early Monday morning. Had they walked a bit further they would have seen two massive fireplaces in the Lounge Bar ornamented with copper kettles and frying pans and above the bar itself, two old pistols fixed on the wall as if ready to duel. The whole rambling building was steeped in history and full of atmosphere.

There was a large bowl of pot pourri on the mahogany reception desk. It exuded a faint musky perfume which complemented the last vestiges of dinner clinging to the air and blended with the lingering notes of stale beer. Behind the desk, waiting for them to arrive, was a receptionist, dressed in a crisp white blouse, navy waistcoat and skirt. "Good evening. Mr and Mrs. Chisholm?"

"That's right," Ian said as he let go of the suitcases and shuffled them out of the way under the overhang of the counter. Pippa had gone quiet. She was savouring their new partnership title.

"Did you have a good journey?"

"Fine, thanks. We haven't come far."

"That's good." The receptionist pushed a key on a large black plastic fob over the desk towards Ian. "Here's your key. I just need a couple of signatures, please. Do you need help with your luggage?"

Ian shook his head. "We haven't got much. Where do I sign?"

He had booked The Queen's Suite for the night and the minute Pippa walked in through the door she was enchanted. The room had lattice windows, a big four poster bed with its tester held up by some sturdy barley twist posts and the floor was covered wall to wall, by a deep pink carpet. She put her bag and jacket down onto a matching pink-covered chair and the minute Ian let go of the suitcases and closed the door behind him, she rushed over to give him a hug. "This is a lovely, lovely room and you are a lovely, lovely man," she said and then an unsettling thought occurred to her. "There aren't any ghosts in here, are there?"

He gave her a sinister smile. "Only the Golden Lady who appears in the Residents' Lounge and a few Tudor spectres which materialise now and again when the fancy takes them."

She giggled. "You're not so lovely after all. You know just how to make a girl feel safe." She was not quite sure whether to believe him or not. "The hotel is a bit spooky."

"Of course it's spooky. It's very old. Good Queen Bess visited here you know."

Pippa was prepared to be impressed. "Did she?"

"Yes. She was supposed to have been in this very room, actually. According to the brochure the hotel sent me she was served with, '*three oxen and one hundred and fortie geese*' for breakfast. I don't think you'd better have an enormous breakfast tomorrow morning though, SweetP."

"Why ever not? We are on holiday aren't we? Are we in a hurry to leave, tomorrow? Come on, tell me. Where *are* we going Ian?"

"Oh, all right. How are your sea-legs?"

"Fine. I'm a great sailor," Pippa declared, gamely. "Are we going sailing, then?"

"Not exactly," he said, unwilling to give anything away. "I'll give you another clue. Southampton."

Pippa's eyes shone, "I know, you've booked us on a cruise haven't you?"

"Yes I have, but where to?"

"The Canary Isles?" Ian shook his head. Pippa tried a second time. "The Caribbean?"

"Nope. This could take us all night and I've got much better things to do." Ian grinned at her. "It's a cruise to the Norwegian Fjords. We're going to see … *Sognefjord, Nordfjord and Geirangerfjord where you can watch shadows cast by the setting sun gently dance across the glass-like water…* How about that? Romantic enough for you? I've also booked us a cabin with a balcony so that we can see where we're going and each morning we can have an al fresco breakfast with a different view. To cap it all I've booked us a personal butler service too." He put his hands on her waist. "Are you pleased, my wonderful wife?"

Pippa had been stunned into silence for a brief moment but her face revealed what she was thinking. "Pleased? I'm delighted. I'm glad I asked you to surprise me. I would never in a million years have thought up such a wonderful and romantic trip. I was so sure the car was the best surprise yet, but I was wrong. A cruise beats that hands down. I hope you haven't peaked too soon, surprise-wise," she said, kissing him enthusiastically and leaving him with just enough breath to inform her that there were plenty more surprises to come.

The first surprise that awaited them though, was a fairly unpleasant one. Pippa's sea-legs turned out to be not as sturdy as she had imagined and on a couple of mornings during the cruise she woke up feeling decidedly queasy. However, being made of stern stuff, she tried not to complain too much. The malaise had always passed by lunch-time and as it did not hamper their sight-seeing in any way, it was soon forgotten.

Back in Linchester everything had gone rather flat. The wedding that had been anticipated, meticulously planned and then enjoyed by all, was now over. All the excitement had dissipated and the sense of anti-climax increased in direct proportion to the stripping bare of the marquee.

While the newly-weds were on honeymoon, Adrian and Isobel were staying at twenty-seven Blain Gardens with Edith, to look after Millie. They were all enjoying their short break in Linchester. Edith had been pottering about in the garden to her heart's content and making batches of scones to pass the time. They had planned a trip to Bosham to take in the sea view and have some lunch at a café they knew there, which overlooked the harbour. They also intended to visit the Spinnaker Tower in Portsmouth where Pippa had received her romantic proposal of marriage.

They had been given an open invitation to take tea with Ivy whenever they wanted and Edith had already been next door. They all realised that the week was going to pass quickly and before they knew it, Ian and Pippa would be back to pick up the stitches of their old life and to knit together their brand new one. So much for the Flynns of Hardale.

The Chisholms of Symington, however, were not on holiday. Neither were they going to have much of a lull in their lives. As soon as the marquee had finally disappeared from their back garden they were to be faced with a dilemma which would guarantee them no peace of mind for some time to come.

6

Jane emerged from the shower. Gingerly, she stepped out of the bath. One foot on the mat, she reached for a towel, gave her short, dark, hair a perfunctory rub and then dealt with the rest of her body in a similar fashion. She dressed with the minimum amount of fuss, her mind elsewhere.

The bathroom window was half-open and crows in the nearby wood could be heard completing their early morning debriefing session, calling to each other in their raucous fashion like old men, their voices gravelled by years of Capstan Full Strength. Jane did not notice. She did not even notice the draught coming in through that same window which was making Gaynor's carefully tended spider plant lift and wave its long, thin, fronds as if to some unheard music like an exotic dancer weaving diaphanous scarves into intricate patterns above her head.

She did not notice her immediate surroundings because her mind was on the future. She was thinking of her meeting with Fr. Philip. After she had seen him, she had made up her mind to broach the subject with her mother. Telling her father could wait for another day or two. It could wait until she had screwed up enough courage to weather the storm that would surely blow up as a consequence of her revelation; her heart was lighter now she had mentioned the unmentionable and even that trial no longer had the power to crush her.

She wondered if Susie would laugh when she found out and then realised that Susie's opinion was irrelevant. She was absolutely convinced she was being called to the priesthood and no-one and nothing was going to deflect her from that.

She left the house in due course, merely informing her mother that she was, "Just going out". Nothing more and nothing less. Gaynor did not quiz her as to her intended destination. She trusted her. Her eldest daughter had never given her a moment's cause for concern. She had never massaged the truth and had always returned home when expected, having been precisely where she had said she was going. In fact, Jane had always been what others might describe as an easy child; unlike her sister, who had given her parents no end of anxious moments.

Susie's childhood and teenage years had been liberally sprinkled with scrapes and later than late nights, followed by illicit lie-ins due to the fact that her internal body clock seemed to have lost its batteries. No-one was more surprised than Gaynor when she had applied for, and been offered, a place at university to study Drama and Media Studies and had then accepted it.

In fact, so completely unaware of the hornet's nest Jane was about to stir up was she, that she called out an airy, "Goodbye," to her daughter as she left the house and then thought no more about it. She had merely carried on loading up her car with Ian and Pippa's wedding presents so that she could deliver them to twenty-seven Blain Gardens later on that morning.

The parish office was small and well-equipped. It was a late addition to the church hall and had been provided with its own private door. The walls were lined with shelves stuffed full of books of every size, shape and colour, on topics of an eclectic but erudite nature. The desk, which was carefully placed directly under the small window over-looking the vicarage, managed to support not only a telephone but also a photocopier, a computer and two loud speakers. Fr. Philip was well known for his love of seventies music and in particular *Frank Zappa*, whose music he used for inspiration while he thought up one of his witty and scholarly sermons.

Jane presented herself promptly at ten o'clock, as arranged, to find Fr. Philip waiting for her. "Ah, Jane," he said. "Come in and sit down."

She gave him a shy, "Hello," and then sat down, folded her hands on her knees and lowered her eyes. Now the moment had come, she was not quite sure how to begin.

Fr. Philip was a kind man and well-known for his inter-personal skills. He realised straight away that Jane felt a mite self-conscious and tried to put her at her ease.

"Did you enjoy the reception?"

"Yes." Her eyes stayed glued to the black rug which almost covered the floor.

"There was a lovely atmosphere in the marquee." She nodded, noticing a small threadbare patch under the desk where his feet habitually rested as he pored over his tracts.

"Well, I've thought about our conversation on Sunday and I've looked out some books for you to borrow. If your heart is completely set on this course, that's where you should start."

Jane looked up at him, a grateful smile curving her lips. "Thank you."

"What have you been studying at uni?"

"Psychology."

"Oh good," Fr. Philip said, a twinkle in his eye, "You're going to need a lot of that in our line of work."

Jane felt another smile creeping up on her and finally, she found the courage to ask the question that had been going round and round in her head for the previous twelve months. "Do you think I'm good enough? I realise I've got a long way to go to qualify but I'm not scared of hard work. I'm very sure it's what I'm meant to do. I'm just worried about everyone else's reaction … particularly my father's. Does that make me a bad person?"

"Of course not," he said reassuringly. "It always takes friction to polish anything properly, you know. Right. Let's get back to basics. What makes you so sure this is what you really want to do with your life? How did it all come about in the first place? I need to have some idea for when I have a word with the powers that be on your behalf."

Jane thought for a moment. "It all sort of happened gradually, I suppose," she said. "No road to Damascus moment for me, I'm afraid. Gran used to take me to church with her when I was little and I loved going. In fact Susie and I came to Sunday school at this church and we were both confirmed here. Susie sort of drifted away and I started going to the Evangelical church down by the by-pass. Peer pressure, I guess. A lot of my friends went." Jane smiled ruefully. "It wasn't cool to go to church with your grandmother. Anyway, I've always had a strong faith and when I went to York, the first thing I did was to join the Christian Union.

"Good, good," Fr. Philip said. "Have you any idea where your ministry might take you?"

"Not really. Well, that's not quite true. I suppose I have some idea. Before I went to uni I spent a gap year in Africa. I was teaching English in a small school there. I think that's what gave Dad the idea that I should take up teaching as a career, but I know I don't want to do that. I do want my ministry to be with young people, though. There was a strong Christian ethic to everything they did in that school and I thought it was amazing how the little ones could sing hymns, even though most of them couldn't even read. I think I relate to children quite well. At least," she finished hesitantly, "I … like working with them."

Fr. Philip seemed pleased. "Bravo," he said. "*Train up a child in the way he should go: and when he is old, he will not depart from it*, Proverbs, 22:6. Full marks for enthusiasm. Well, I will set the ball rolling for you and for starters, I've put a list of all our services in one of the books so that you'll be able to join us at St. Jude's on a regular basis."

"I'm really grateful. Thanks." Jane took the books from the desk and got up to leave.

"Good luck with your Dad, but I'm sure you won't need it. I knew your grandmother very well and I had a lot of time for her. Actually, I think you have her eyes."

Jane looked pleased. "Everyone says that," she said. "Uncle Ian gave me her Bible after she died. It's well worn, but it's the one I always use now. I'm sorry I never mentioned any of this to her. I know she would have backed me up."

"Don't worry," Fr. Philip said. "We always think the things we are dreading, will be worse than they actually are. Onward and upward." He got up from his chair and opened the door for her. "Don't expect to hear anything straight away. You'll learn that the church takes its time in all things. I can't see that I'll have any news for you by Sunday, but you never know. See you then."

"Yes, I'll be there and thank you again. Very much."

Jane felt wonderful. Light as air. As if she could float above the pavement should a sudden breeze spring up from nowhere. After months of wondering and worrying, she was now working towards her goal. Her secret would soon be out and then everyone would know what it was she wanted to do with the rest of her life.

7

"This is positively the last one," Gaynor said as she heaved an unwieldy package out of the back of her car and carried it in through the front door of twenty-seven Blain Gardens. "It weighs a ton. I can't imagine what it is. They must have used up several pieces of wrapping paper to cover the box." She deposited the parcel on the dining room floor with a sigh of relief.

Isobel was intrigued. "Who's it from?" she asked. "Let's have a look."

"I read the label before I put it in the car," Gaynor said. "It's from Garth, Chrissie and the boys. Did you get round to meeting them at the wedding? Garth's Ian's best friend. Chrissie was wearing that gorgeous gold sari and they have two adorable little boys. Twins. I wonder what it is?"

"I think Pippa pointed them out to me, but I met so many people on Sunday that I couldn't say for sure. I can't imagine what's in there. Something big. We'll just have to wait until they get back to find out, won't we? People have been so generous," Isobel said as she stacked up the last of the smaller presents on the sideboard. "They should be home Sunday night and then, all being well, we're back off up north on Monday morning. I'd love to know where they've gone, wouldn't you?"

"Yes, I would. Ian didn't give anyone a hint as to where they would end up and for once, Mike didn't badger him about it because he was too involved with getting his speech right. July is such a lovely month to get married, don't you think?"

"I suppose it is."

"Flowers everywhere. Trees full of leaves. Balmy nights," Gaynor said reflectively. "We were married in July. It will be our silver wedding anniversary next year."

"Well done," Isobel said. Gaynor did not reply. Her phone was singing a rather muffled *Yankee Doodle* from her bag. "Sorry," she said after she had looked to see who was calling. "I'll have to take this. Hello … Yes. Are you at the library? … Ok. In about fifteen minutes then." She flipped her phone shut. "No peace for the wicked," she said with a little sigh. "That was Jane. She needs a lift home."

"Children," Isobel said, giving Gaynor a sympathetic smile, "Where would we be without them?"

"She can wait a few minutes, I'd just like to say goodbye to your mum before I leave. I probably won't see her again before you go back home."

"She's in the garden. Dead-heading roses probably and having a chat with Ivy. Every time Mum goes out there, Ivy's head appears over the fence. They've become quite friendly over the past few days."

"That's nice. It's not often you make new friends at their age."

"No. I think they might stay in touch. My mum doesn't get out much now. Maybe they'll write to each other. They could speak on the phone; share the odd piece of news. It all helps."

"Ivy was great friends with Ian's mum. Vera dying left a big gap in her life."

"There you are then. It'll be therapeutic for both of them."

When Gaynor finally arrived at the library, her fifteen minutes had stretched to forty-five. She had been inveigled into drinking a quick cup of coffee with Isobel and had then been persuaded to wait for Adrian to return from his walk with Millie before she left. For Jane those minutes had turned into an eternity and she had practiced what she was planning to say to her mother so many times, that her head was spinning. So much so, that when her personal taxi cab eventually drew to a halt in the parking bay outside the library, she could no longer remember how it was she had decided to start.

She put her books down on the back seat with her bag and then climbed into the car beside her mother. "You were a long time."

"Yes. Sorry. I was dropping off the wedding presents." Through the rear view mirror, Gaynor noticed the pile of books on the back seat. "Your exams are over now, you know. You don't need to do any more studying."

"Well, that's where you're wrong, Mum. I do need to study a bit more actually. I... er... I... want to be ordained." She had prepared a much more gradual introduction to her bombshell, but in the end the unexpected piece of news had decided to announce itself, in its own way.

As luck would have it, Gaynor had not released the handbrake. She was waiting for Jane to do up her seatbelt and all she could do was stare at her daughter, open-mouthed. "But we don't even go to church," she said eventually and rather irrelevantly.

"I do," Jane said in a small voice.

Gaynor focussed on letting the brake go and encouraging the car to move. Concentrating on that, seemed preferable to reacting in an adverse fashion to her daughter's startling news. She drove home in silence, trying to work out what she really felt about her becoming a priest. It was barely a ten minute drive to

Symington but thoughts were jostling with one another in her head the whole time.

Pictures of Jane flashed in and out of her mind's eye. Jane as a contemplative and caring little girl. Jane as a teenager, collecting money for the homeless; getting the family to sponsor a cow in Africa. Her anxious face as she revealed her unexpected news. She slowed at a cross roads and turned right.

The jumbled snapshots continued. She could see Jane happily trotting off to Sunday school with Vera Chisholm. She remembered the gap year she had spent in Africa and how much she seemed to have grown up by the time she had returned home. She also recalled the Christian summer camps she had attended; the friendships she had made there; the special bracelets she had worn day after day as a witness to her faith.

She overtook a lumbering blue tractor and made a final left turn. By the time they arrived back outside Migay Lodge, the mental documentary had played itself out and had left her feeling impatient with herself for not having realised much earlier, how her daughter was thinking. She should have known that Jane might want to follow a career in the church. If she really did feel that way, who was she to stop her? This thought brought tears of pride to her eyes, which Jane noticed the minute she turned to face her and immediately misunderstood. She broke the silence. "Oh, Mum. I'm sorry if you're disappointed, but I'm absolutely certain this is what I want to do with the rest of my life. How can I make you understand?"

Gaynor took her daughter's hand in hers. She cleared her throat. "I do understand and I'm not disappointed. I'm proud of you. I should have known you were thinking this way. I don't know what Dad's going to say, though.

He won't be happy. He'd set his heart on you being a teacher."

"I know," Jane said. "I will be a teacher; sort of. I was hoping you'd put in a word for me. Not just yet, though. I'd like a few days to work out the best way to tell him. I think Uncle Ian has already guessed what I want to do because we had a very strange conversation at the reception. He seemed to know exactly what I was thinking. I'd like to wait until he comes back from his honeymoon before I tell Dad. I need as many people as possible to back me up. I'm not going to change my mind, but you know what Dad's like."

Gaynor knew only too well. "It's going to be difficult keeping it from him. We usually discuss everything with each other."

"Please, Mum. I want to do this right," Jane said earnestly.

Gaynor was watching her daughter's face. She thought for a moment. "Oh, all right. I might just give him a few gentle hints, though. Or, at the very least, tell him you're not keen on teaching."

Jane decided to accept her mother's compromise. "Ok."

Gaynor had another thought. "What about Susie?"

"I'm not bothered about Susie. She's the least of my worries." Jane had learned to live with her sister's banter and she was sure she could take a lot more of it if necessary. "She won't be back from Tania's until the weekend. I'll talk to her then." She was now beginning to feel slightly more confident. Pleased that at least her mother was on side. Perhaps Fr. Philip was right. Telling her father might not, after all, be as bad as she had thought.

That evening, Gaynor decided to ring her mother. With Mike out at a Linchester Wanderers committee meeting and Jane ensconced in her bedroom with a DVD and a generous helping of popcorn, she knew she would be able to have a mother and daughter heart-to-heart without interruptions.

Gaynor was an only child. Her mother had suffered a succession of miscarriages before her birth. Her final pregnancy, when Gaynor was just a toddler, which had been swiftly followed by a hysterectomy due to complications at the birth, had resulted in a baby boy who had only survived for a few hours. With no siblings to cramp her style, Gaynor had always had her mother's undivided attention as a child and nothing had changed with the passing years.

Gwynne Roberts and her husband, Lol, were originally from South Wales. They had moved to Linchester due to his work on the railways and although they still kept their ties with the Valleys, Gwynne and Lol had chosen to stay put, living only a stone's throw from Gaynor and Mike in a small but attractive flat, part of a converted Edwardian country house, which was, coincidentally, one of Chisholm Construction's first big projects.

Lol was a small wiry Welshman with eyes of ebony and an impressive aquiline nose. He had been a great athlete in his youth and despite his age he still liked to jog on a regular basis. Unlike his wife, whose accent had been slightly softened by her years in the south of England, the minute he opened his mouth, his heritage could not be denied. His terms of endearment were Welsh; his collection of Max Boyce recordings, legendary and the first of March each year found him sporting a daffodil somewhere about his person.

Gwynne did not share her husband's love of physical activity, to which her ample proportions bore irrefutable witness, but she did enjoy knitting. This made her Christmas presents for all the family somewhat predictable. Mike had a fine selection of her stripy bobble hats and fingerless mittens, not to mention some warm knitted socks, for which he was truly grateful. A building site in winter can be a very bleak place indeed. He got on well with his in-laws, particularly his father-in-law, despite Lol's fanatical support of the Welsh rugby team and Mike's predilection for football in general and Linchester Wanderers in particular. This was just as well, because they saw each other often. Gwynne and Lol were both frequent visitors to Migay Lodge and Gaynor and her mother went shopping together most weeks.

"Have you got time for a chat, Mum?" Gaynor asked after the usual niceties had been observed.

"Yes, of course. Do you want to go over the wedding again?"

"No. It's not that, Mum. It's Jane."

"What has Jane been up to? Oh I know, she's got her results at last. How did she do? Has she found a job yet?"

"No, no. Nothing like that." Gaynor was amused at her mother's keen interest in Jane's affairs, "But she has decided what she wants to do with her life."

"Oh good. What is it?" her mother asked eagerly.

"Well, you're not going to believe this, but she wants to be ordained a priest," she said and then waited for the sharp intake of breath.

"Well I never. There's a surprise," her mother said mildly and with more than a hint of the Rhondda in her voice.

"Is that all you've got to say, Mum?" Gaynor asked. She had expected shock at least and possibly horror and alarm to follow shortly afterwards.

"Why? What do you want me to say? Religion is in the genes, my pet. All the Parrys were devout chapel-goers. Your great uncle Caradoc was a minister you know, as was his father before him. Granted they were *men*, but that's a minor detail. From what I've read, she'll be fine as long as she doesn't want to be a bishop."

"You are priceless, Mum," Gaynor said, smiling in spite of herself. "I didn't know anything about a great uncle being a minister. Tell me more." She was both fascinated and relieved at her mother's revelation. At the very least it was an interesting piece of family folk lore which had so far escaped her notice and at best, it would be good ammunition to use against Mike, should he make too much of a fuss about Jane.

Gwynne was a great story teller. She kept Gaynor amused for almost an hour with one family anecdote after another and only brought the conversation to an end after her husband came to remind her that it was time for a programme she had been waiting to watch on the television. "Send my love to Janie, won't you my sweet? And let me know as soon as those results are out. Speak to you soon."

Gaynor came away from the telephone with her head full of good thoughts. There was absolutely no need for her to worry about Jane and her future plans. Telling Mike about it should not be a problem. It was whatever he might say, in the Parry/Roberts genes and he could not argue with that.

Mike's thoughts a few days later were not so sanguine. He had a problem. He had paid to have his regular Health and Safety checks carried out at the old airfield site, which was perfectly normal practice. He had not been expecting any trouble with it and, sure enough, the inspectors were satisfied with everything there. However, they warned him that the Health and Safety Executive were doing their own spot checks in the Linchester area and he found out a few days later that Chisholm Construction had been selected for one of these visits. On the Friday before Ian and Pippa's return from honeymoon, an inspector called at the old airfield site and issue was taken with some of the scaffolding.

In a rash moment, Ian had volunteered to deal with any such problems should they arise and now one had been discovered while he was inconveniently away, Mike was not happy. He returned home that night, fuming. The way he opened the front door alerted Gaynor to his bad mood and as the hinges protested at their rough treatment, she took a deep breath and waited.

"When's he due back?" Mike said as soon as he entered the kitchen.

"Hello, dear. Not a good day, today?" she asked him calmly. "I suppose you mean Ian."

Mike was impatient. "Of course I mean Ian. Who else would I mean? Honeymoons should be banned. I didn't expect him to be on holiday the whole time when I asked him to work with me on this project. How am I supposed to run a business with half the work force taking time off every five minutes?"

Gaynor was used to dealing with Mike's outbursts. "Here's a cup of tea," she said. "Supper will be ready in half an hour. Ian will be back at work on Monday and he can deal with the problem then, whatever it is. It's the weekend now. You can forget all about Chisholm Construction for a couple of days and have a nice rest."

Mike was not to be so easily placated. "A nice rest?" he said, his voice rising again. "How can I possibly have a rest, with all this on my mind?"

Gaynor concentrated on buffing up the shine on her already immaculate kettle and refused to be drawn into her husband's inner turmoil. Eventually, after a few more blistering comments and with his food finally in front of him, Mike settled down to eat his meal.

She left him to it, thinking to herself that it was annoying a major problem should have blown up at the building site, just when they all needed Mike to be calm and receptive to Jane's equally challenging news. She comforted herself with the knowledge that she had a full bottle of Bach's Rescue Remedy in her handbag and a brand new packet of Camomile tea in the kitchen cupboard. She had a feeling she would need to resort to both of these, before the week was out.

8

Ian and Pippa returned to Southampton on Sunday evening unaware that a large quantity of feathers were about to fly and not just from one bird, either. They had enjoyed their cruise, but Pippa was glad to return to land so that her faulty sea-legs could be dispensed with. "It's good to be back," she said. "Not that I haven't enjoyed the trip, but I think I prefer something solid under my feet."

"I wonder what's been going on at home," Ian said as he drove through Hampshire at a smart pace.

Pippa was weary. She pushed her neck back against the head-rest and shut her eyes. "Not much, I don't suppose. Ivy will have been offering numerous cups of tea to all and sundry. Mike will have been complaining about the mess the marquee has left on his lawn. Gaynor will have been pouring oil on troubled waters and I expect Gran's been baking. D'you mind if I nod off for a bit? I don't know why I'm so sleepy."

Ian smiled at Pippa's thumbnail sketch of Linchester life. "It must be all the sea air we've had," he said. "Nod away. I'll wake you up as soon as we get off the dual carriageway. That way you'll have plenty of time to gather your thoughts before our debriefing session. Your Mum'll be bound to want to know every last little detail of our holiday."

Isobel, Edith and Adrian had all been to church with Ivy that morning and had spent the rest of the day preparing for the honeymooners' return. "I reckon they've gone to Paris," Adrian said as he helped Isobel lay the table that evening. "Ian seems keen on towers."

"No. I think it has to be the Greek islands. Much more romantic. What d'you think, Mum?"

"I wouldn't know. I just hope they get back safely."

Millie had picked up on all the excitement in the house and she would not settle down anywhere. In the end Adrian took her out for a long walk, which finally got rid of her excess energy. At seven o'clock she was fast asleep in her basket under the kitchen table.

"Wake up, SweetP. We're just passing the big roundabout." Ian gave Pippa's knee a couple of taps.

She awoke with a start and wondered where she was for a minute, "Thank goodness you woke me," she said. "I can't imagine how I would have coped with all those puppies."

Ian took his eyes off the road for a second to give her a blank stare. "What on earth are you talking about?" The car reduced speed as they approached the roundabout and then, taking the first exit, it headed for Blain Gardens.

"I was just dreaming about Millie having loads and loads of puppies. Each time she barked, another one popped out. What d'you think it means?"

He laughed. "I think it means we should have her spayed. Well, here we are. Shall I carry you over the threshold, SweetP?"

"You'd better not. After all those delicious meals we've had I must weigh a ton. Just look at my stomach," said Pippa, in mock despair.

"Every inch of you is adorable," Ian said and he snatched a quick kiss before she got out of the car.

"Well, we've all seen pictures of the fjords, but nothing really prepares you for the magnificence of them in real life, Mum," Pippa said as they relaxed round the table after their meal. "You should have seen all those green hillsides and the towering mountains. They were enormous; they actually seemed to disappear into the clouds. And the clapboard houses. They were painted all the colours of the rainbow and there were sweet little villages built right up against the water's edge. As the sun set each evening there we were, on our own private balcony, watching the shadows cast by the mountains getting longer and longer and the stars beginning to peep through the velvety black sky." She sighed. "It was quite magical, wasn't it, Ian?"

"It certainly seemed unreal. Like living on a film set. The scenery was amazing."

"It sounds wonderful," Isobel said, her artist's eye seeing the picture painted by Pippa's expressive words. "Perhaps we should go to Norway, darling."

"Why not? We won't be able to take the dogs with us, though, will we?"

"*Pas de problème*," she said with a Gallic wave of her arms. "I'm sure Will Grace will look after them for us."

Adrian thought this a strange role reversal. It was usually Isobel who was super-sensitive to their Lakeland terriers' needs, not him. He found Nip and Tuck's noisy antics somewhat tiresome.

"Well, I won't be going," Edith said. "I will just have to make do with the photos. You did have time to take some, I hope?" She had enjoyed her stay in Blain Gardens and her time with Ivy. She had forgotten how good it was to chat with someone her own age who remembered all the things she did.

She had decided a long time ago that old age was a trial. Particularly so when most of your friends had passed away before you and there were none of your contemporaries left to call you by your first name; no-one with whom to reminisce. Not long after their first meeting, Edith and Ivy had discovered they had a great deal in common. A firm friendship had been cemented and, as Isobel had predicted, they had promised to stay in touch with each other when Edith returned home to Hardale.

"Of course we did, Gran." Pippa glanced across the room to the pile of unopened wedding gifts in the corner. "You'll have to wait for those, though. Ian needs to download them onto his computer. Any more questions or can we open our presents, now?"

"Yes. What a good idea. Open them. This one first," Isobel said. She was standing beside Garth and Chrissie's offering. "I'm dying to know what's in it."

Ian eyed up the parcel. "Is it from Garth and Chrissie?" he asked.

"Yes."

"In that case I know what it is."

"So do I," Pippa said, tearing off the Sellotape with relish. She giggled. "I hope you haven't used up all the flour on your scones, Gran."

"How did you know I'd been baking?"

"Just a guess."

"Anyway, I bought you some more," Edith said. "Why?"

"I think we're going to need it."

The last sheet of paper fell to the floor and Isobel's curiosity was satisfied at last.

"It's a bread maker," she said in surprise.

Adrian seemed pleased. "Oh good," he said. "Home-made bread for breakfast, then. Just what we need to set us up for the journey home."

9

Wednesday was the day Jane had settled upon to reveal all. She reckoned she should have her exam results by then and Ian would be back at work and able to play his part as backstop in the verbal rounders game she would be engaged in with her father. She expected him to be aiming the ball at all her bases and she needed a good team behind her. Gaynor would be fielding any shots that went wide and she hoped she could persuade her sister to act as first reserve.

Susie returned home from her friend's house late Sunday afternoon and Jane decided to talk to her after supper. Gaynor had engineered an evening out with Mike so that the two girls could be alone in the house, giving Jane a chance to discuss things with Susie in peace.

So, that evening, shortly after eight o'clock, she mounted the stairs to Susie's bedroom carrying with her a tray full of tempting goodies. She balanced the tray on her knee and knocked on the door. She knew her sister would find it impossible to resist the glass of wine, juicy strawberries and large bag of Minstrels she had discovered in the kitchen cupboard and she hoped they would, at the very least, put Susie in a receptive mood.

"Can we have a chat, Suze?" she asked tentatively, pushing the door open with her elbow.

"Sure, what's up?" Susie asked, half an ear on her radio.

"I've got something to tell you."

Jane edged the tray carefully onto a corner of her sister's overflowing dressing table. It was heaped high with pots of cosmetics, a pint glass of half-drunk water, several strings of colourful beads, a boudoir box of paper hankies and, suspended from the mirror by their laces, a pair of seriously muddy hiking boots.

It was difficult to see the grey carpet under the morass of unread reference books and well-thumbed magazines, not to mention the pile of discarded clothes on the top of which lay two pairs of Audrey Hepburn-style sunglasses. Jane cleared herself a space without comment and then, helping herself to a glass of wine first, she sat down on the floor.

"Mmm, Minstrels, strawberries *and* wine. This must be important." Susie popped a small but juicy strawberry into her mouth and turned, briefly, to face her sister. "Right, spill."

"I know what I'm going to do now I've left uni."

"Do you, now," Susie said, not completely engaging with the conversation as she searched for an emery board.

"I want to be ordained."

"Ordained? What d'you mean?" Susie's mouth was now full of chocolates coated in a *crisp candy shell*, each one of which she had bitten in half before taking another. She was not looking at Jane, but filing the fingernails of her left hand with the utmost care.

Jane stayed perfectly calm. "I want to become a priest," she said, hoping that her sister would now pay more attention.

Susie looked up from her nails. "What on earth d'you want to do that for? You'll have to preach sermons. You know you're no good at performing," she said with sisterly candour. "You'll never have a weekend off either." She thought for a moment. "Yes and worse than that, you'll have to wear those awful black robes all the time."

"Oh, dear. This isn't a very good start," Jane said. If she could not explain herself to her sister, what chance did she have with her father? "Look, it's not about clothes, Suze and I'm sure I can learn to give sermons. There must be a technique to it. It's about conviction and vocation. I want to serve as a priest. It's what I'm meant to do, I know it. I really, really, want you to understand."

Susie shrugged her shoulders, "Well, I don't understand. I do remember you sorting out funeral services for our guinea pigs when they died and you do seem to go to church an awful lot, I suppose. What does Dad think about it?"

"He doesn't know yet. I wanted to tell you first," Jane said. She was not quite sure how Susie was taking her news. Had she won her over? At least she hadn't laughed.

"O-oh," Susie said, "Tut, tut, Janie. He won't be pleased you know. I thought you were going to teach. I think he thought you were too."

"I will be teaching, won't I? Sort of. But I'll also be serving, praying, praising, preaching, ministering, baptising and … well I don't know what else. I haven't started the training yet. All I know is, I feel as if I'm being called. I *have* to do it. Whether Dad likes it or not; or you, come to that." Jane took a large gulp of wine from her glass and swallowed it quickly. There. She had stated her case clearly, so there could be no misunderstanding and her eyes were glowing with fervour, daring her sister to contradict her.

Susie stopped filing her nails. She switched off the radio and helped herself to her glass of wine. She also took a sip, but swilled it thoughtfully round her tongue before she let it slide silkily down her throat. She had listened carefully to the words coming out of her sister's mouth. She had seen how Jane's eyes had come alive as she was explaining everything; she recognised sincerity when she saw it. She reckoned this was seriously grown-up stuff and words played no part in what she was feeling, so she said nothing. She got up from her bed where she had been sitting cross-legged and simply gave Jane a big hug, which was all that was necessary really.

In the soft silence of the room, Jane knew she had got through to Susie and Susie knew that Jane wanted this more than anything else in the whole world. Her sister's conviction shone through and it was awesome. Although she would never understand it, she did wholeheartedly respect it.

Meanwhile, elsewhere, Gaynor had decided to smooth Jane's path by sowing a few seeds in Mike's head. "You know Jane's results should be through by Wednesday?"

"Yes. What d'you think she'll do next? She really needs a job over the summer while she applies for teacher training courses."

"I don't think that's going to happen, Mike. She doesn't want to go into teaching."

"Really? Why not? They're always banging on about a shortage of teachers. The pay's good and the holidays. She'd never be out of a job. She's a hard worker and she's got a good brain on her. She loves children. I think she'd make a great teacher."

"Maybe, but her qualifications for the job are not the issue here. She really doesn't want to do it."

"That's silly. She hasn't even looked into it yet. She hasn't thought it through. I can just see her as head teacher of a primary school, somewhere. I'll have a word with her. Explain what a good idea it is. Make her understand."

"You don't get to be a head teacher, straight from university."

"I suppose not, but in time …"

"Time's not the issue, here."

"No, but if she just gave it a try? That's all I'm saying."

Gaynor was determined to make her point. "Haven't you heard a word of what I've been saying, Mike? No one should start something they don't intend to finish."

"Oh, all right," he said. He had noticed Gaynor's disapproving expression and recognised her tone of voice. He finally decided to accept what she was trying to tell him. "What else could she do then?"

"I'm not sure, but it's not for us to say, is it? It's Janie's life after all. I expect she's got some sort of a plan in mind."

"She hasn't said anything to me about a plan."

Gaynor wavered. She wanted to tell him. Looking down at her martini, she poked at the cherry with her cocktail stick, avoiding his eyes. He would find out soon enough and she had promised. "No. Well, we'll just have to wait until she does, won't we?"

10

"It's a boy," Simon said, sounding paradoxically exhausted and jubilant at the same time.

"Well done. Congratulations. Is everything alright?" Ian asked after he had mouthed, *Simon,* to Pippa. She was on her way out of the front door when the telephone rang on Wednesday morning and she back-tracked immediately.

"He was a bit early wasn't he? Wait a minute; Pippa's desperate to talk to you." Ian relinquished the hand set to Pippa. She snatched it greedily. She wanted to know everything, but most of all, she wanted to find out when she could go and visit Alice.

She waited while Simon went through all the gory details. "Took a while then? Poor Alice. When's visiting?"

"Any afternoon, after two. Don't you want to know what we've called him?"

"At a rough guess, I'd say it's *not* Maximilian."

"No chance. We've settled on Oliver actually. He is *so* small, Pippa and very fair like his Mum. All his little fingers and toes are there. I can't believe it. Alice is very tired, but she told me to tell you to go in and see her as soon as you can."

"I can't wait to see her and meet Oliver. I don't think I'm very busy today. I could probably go in this afternoon. I'll check my diary when I get to work and text you. It's lovely news. Thanks for letting us know so quickly."

"Alice insisted. She's given me a list of about fifty people to ring and you and Ian were number three. Now I've got to tell the rest of them. It'll probably take me all morning."

Pippa giggled. "I'd better let you go, then." She put the phone down. "What a nice way to start the day. I'll pop into the one-stop and get them a card before I go into work."

"Hold on a sec. Perhaps you'd better get a card for Jane as well, while you're in there."

"Yes. I hadn't forgotten that today's the day. What time does Mike's post arrive?"

"I haven't a clue. Knowing Mike, I'm sure he'll ring the minute it does. I hope Jane's not too nervous. She seemed quite worried when I spoke to her at the reception."

"Let me know as soon as you find out, won't you? I could do with not going to work this morning. I still feel quite tired. Perhaps we should have taken an extra week off to get over the honeymoon. Aren't you tired?"

"No, I feel full of energy," Ian said with a grin, running on the spot just to prove his point. "I think marriage agrees with me."

Pippa laughed, kissed him goodbye and set off for the auction rooms. She was beginning to be worried about her lack of energy. It was not like her at all and she had not entirely left her sea-legs behind in Southampton either. She reckoned that after weeks and weeks of preparation and with all the wedding excitement, she must have used up all her energy reserves.

Jane was sitting all alone in her bedroom, waiting for news and trying to stay calm. Gaynor was in the kitchen, her ears alert for the postman. She ran into the hall as soon as she heard the rattle of the letterbox and the ominous soft thud of envelopes hitting the mat. "Post's here," she called upstairs, making Jane jump. "It's arrived, Janie."

The minute she heard her mother's voice, Jane's teeth started chattering. Her heart was already pulsating in her ears and she emerged from her room all of a quiver. She walked down the stairs as fast as her disobedient legs would allow. "Where's Dad?" she asked, apprehensively.

"In the office, on the phone. Come on, treasure. I'm dying to see how you've done." Gaynor handed the envelope to her reluctant daughter and held her breath.

Jane looked at the envelope. Slowly, she turned it over in her hand. She started to tear it open and then changed her mind, tossing it back to her mother as if it had suddenly become red hot. "I can't, Mum," she said in a strained voice. "You open it for me."

"Are you sure?"

She nodded, silently biting her lip.

"Here we go then," Gaynor said. She ripped open the envelope and removing the sheet of paper inside, she unfolded it, skimmed the words twice to make sure she had understood it correctly and then, barely able to contain her excitement, she gave her daughter the good news. "It's all right. You don't have to worry. You've passed. Well done, Janie. Here, read it for yourself." She handed the letter straight back again, giving her daughter a big hug at the same time.

"It's a two:one. Fantastic. Mum, I've got a two:one." Jane shouted the *two:one* as loud as she could. She grabbed her mother, making her dance an erratic polka up and down the hall with her, chanting, "Two:one, two:one," as they went.

"What's all the noise about?" asked a bleary-eyed Susie who had appeared, tousle-haired, in her skimpy polka dot nightie at the top of the stairs.

"I've got a two:one," Jane cried.

"Wicked," Susie said. She yawned. "Better than a Desmond."

"Desmond?" Mike said as he joined the party in the hall. The cavorting stopped abruptly. He noticed on the floor the discarded letter with the university coat of arms printed at the top of it. "Is that one of your lecturers, Jane? What does he want?" He cast his eyes upwards and took in Susie's state of *déshabille*. "Don't stand there like that. Go and get some clothes on." Susie raised a dismissive hand at him, yawned again and meandered off back to bed.

Gaynor and Jane stood side by side, waiting. The atmosphere seemed charged with the melange of emotions swirling around it, the most tangible being Jane's intermingled ecstatic delight and heartfelt relief. Gaynor's happiness for her daughter and pride in her achievement were somewhat tempered by her anxiety at what her husband might do next.

"I've got my results, Dad. I got a two:one. I'm so pleased."

"That's my girl, of course you did. What's Desmond got to do with it?"

"It's a joke, dear," Gaynor said quietly, well up on student-speak, "If you pass with a two:two it's called a Desmond, a pun on the name Tutu. You know, Bishop Desmond Tutu? But it doesn't matter, because Jane got a two:one anyway."

"Right," Mike said. "So what are you going to do now? Obviously we'll go out for a meal to celebrate or something, but I mean with the rest of your life. Have you thought any more about teaching?"

Gaynor gritted her teeth. "Mike," she said menacingly, but Jane did not mind. She was so pleased with her results that she was immune from his one track mind.

"It's all right, Mum. I've got something to tell you, Dad. I'm not going to be a teacher."

Gaynor caught Jane's eye and shook her head. She was desperately hoping they could enjoy her achievement for a while before her other plans were revealed. Jane ignored her mother's pleading eyes. "I'm going to be a priest."

Mike blanched. He looked at Gaynor, whose face was a blank page and then back to a defiant Jane. Finally he found his voice. "But you can't. You're a girl."

"There are lots of women priests now you know, Dad. It's what I really want to do." She was encouraged by her father's lack of bluster. Her mother knew better.

"Gaye?" Mike said, pathetically.

"Come on," his wife said. She took him by his arm. "I'm going to make you a nice cup of tea."

It took Gaynor nearly an hour to rationalise things for Mike and to calm him down after the initial shock had subsided and his bluster had returned. During this time he said a few things to Jane which he probably should not have said. In the end, she removed herself from his vicinity and left her mother to placate him as best she could.

Gaynor eventually moulded his bruised psyche into something approaching acceptance and left him awash with tea, sitting in his office and staring blankly at his computer screen, while she went to telephone her mother with her mixed bag of news.

"This is just a quick call, Mum. I thought you'd like to know. Jane got a two:one."

"Great. That's excellent news. She's done well, hasn't she? Wait till I tell your Da. He'll be back soon. He *will* be pleased. What did Mike say?"

"Too much, as usual. I think he was pleased at first, but then Jane told him all about the priest thing and he flipped."

"He'll come round, don't you worry. I've got a card all ready for her. I'll get your Da to drop it in when he goes out for his run later. Tell her from me that she's a very clever girl. Oh, before you go, Gaynor, has Pippa's friend had her baby yet? I've finished the little cardi I was making."

"Not as far as I know. I haven't spoken to Pippa for a couple of days. Should be any day now, I think. If I hear anything I'll let you know. I must get back to Mike. Jane could come in any minute and I don't want him upsetting her again."

Gaynor put the phone down and took a deep breath. She felt that her mother was being unduly optimistic. Mike had taken Jane's news badly and she realised that it was going to involve more tough-talking on her part to win him over. Sure enough, as she headed back towards the office, she could hear the plaintive cry of her husband in torment.

"Gaye. *Gaye.* I need to talk to you. Gaye, where *are* you?"

11

"Have you heard anything?" Pippa asked when she rang Ian at lunch-time. "The post must have arrived by now."

"Not yet. Mike's not even here and I've been so busy trying to sort out this scaffolding that I haven't had a chance to ring him."

"I'm going to see Alice in a minute. When are you having your lunch break?"

"In about half an hour. I'll ring him then and text you. Send Alice my love."

"I will and don't forget to tell Gaynor about Alice's baby if you get a chance. I think her Mum's been knitting something for him."

When Ian finally got round to making his call, Mike's mobile was switched off and he had to try the land line. It was Susie who answered.

"Is your Dad there?"

"He is, but we're having a bit of a family crisis at the moment."

"Oh dear. Didn't Jane pass?"

"It's not that. Her results were very good. She got a two:one. She's just told Dad that she doesn't want to be a teacher and he's flipped."

"I see," Ian said and then, on the spur of the moment, he added, "I'm coming round."

He gave himself enough time to send Pippa a quick text as promised and then he set off for his brother's house. When he arrived at Migay Lodge all appeared calm.

It was Gaynor who opened the door and she seemed relieved to see him. "Ian. Thank goodness you're here. Susie told me you rang. I think you know what's been going on."

"Susie told me about Jane's results," Ian said, wondering precisely what it was he was supposed to know.

"I don't mean that. I mean Jane's plans for the future."

"You mean that she doesn't want to be a teacher?"

"Not even that so much as what she wants to do instead."

"Ah," Ian said, knowingly. "Where is she?"

"She's gone for a walk and Mike's in the office, sulking. Could you go and have a word with him?"

"I'll try, but I'm only human. Don't expect too much." He approached the office door and opened it warily, wondering what sort of a reaction he would get. "Good news about Jane," he said.

Mike looked up from his computer. "You've heard, then," he said, looking grim.

"What I've heard, mate, is that your clever daughter has passed her exams with flying colours and she knows what she wants to do with her life. I'd say that was excellent news. What's your problem?"

"It's not normal, that's what. Women aren't meant to be priests," Mike said.

"What is normal? We all have our own dreams and ambitions. Vocations, even. There are quite a few women priests out there now. I think it's impressive she knows what she wants to do with her life. A lot of people her age can't decide. She'll earn a decent wage, have accommodation provided. She'll be helping other people." Ian could tell he was getting nowhere fast, so he tried to lighten the atmosphere. "I think she might even be entitled to a free wedding. That'll save you a bob or two."

Mike looked at his brother, a suspicious frown appearing on his face. "How come you know so much about it? She told you, didn't she?"

"Most of that is common knowledge and nobody told me in so many words. I just guessed. Look," Ian said, beginning to get exasperated by his brother's negative attitude, "She hasn't announced that she's joining a drug trafficking ring, or that she's going on the streets. She wants to be a priest, for heaven's sake."

"All right. I get the message, mate. I've had an earful from Gaynor along the same lines, but she's my little Janie. She's so young. She's going to have to dedicate her life to all of this and it's not a barrel of laughs you know. It's not only preaching to the converted. It involves other people's problems; bereaved families; dead bodies." Mike shuddered.

"It's not all bad, either. Yes, that's part of it, but there's also baptisms and weddings. She'll be spreading the word and in essence, it's teaching, which is what you wanted her to do in the first place. All she's done is to choose a different classroom."

"I suppose," Mike said, unhappily. "Anyhow, I've decided on a plan of action. I've booked Susie and Jane two weeks in the sun and if she's still thinking the same way when she comes back, then I reckon I'll have to go along with it. Two weeks with Susie is enough to try the patience of a saint and it might put her off ministering to others."

Ian wasn't sure this ploy would have the desired effect, but if it kept Mike happy then it was worth a try. "Ok, but don't go on and on about the teaching any more. It's just counter-productive. I'm sure Mum would have been really proud of Jane, I know I am." Having fired his parting shot, Ian left Mike to mull over what he had said.

While Ian had been trying to mollify his brother, Pippa was at the hospital cooing over Alice's brand new baby. "He is absolutely gorgeous," she said as she peeped into the cot beside Alice's bed.

"He is, isn't he?"

"How was it?"

"You don't want to know. I think they've stitched up everything underneath. I can't even walk properly, but he's worth it. I can't believe how clever I am."

Pippa was not really listening. "His fingers are so small," she said. She was surprised at how maternal little Oliver made her feel. "He smells so lovely too."

Alice smiled. "It sounds to me as if you want one yourself."

"I don't think so," Pippa said. "Well not right away, but I must admit he is very sweet. When are you going home?"

"Tomorrow, probably. If I can get the breast feeding sorted. It's not as easy as you think, but I'm going to have a go. Simon thinks we should go the bottle route because he wants to feed the baby all the time. It's really funny, Pippa. I didn't think he'd be all that bothered, but he's like a dog with two tails. Every bit the proud father."

"That's nice. Can I have a cuddle?"

"Of course you can. Mind his head," Alice said as Pippa picked up the baby.

He felt light and warm and alive as he moved in her arms. Pippa was hooked. "Oh, Alice. You're so lucky." She stroked his soft cheek and he made a strange squeaking noise. He turned his head searching for milk, his little mouth soft and pink and open.

"Here, give him back to me," Alice said. "I think he's hungry."

Pippa stayed another half an hour and left the hospital when Simon arrived, armed with an enormous bouquet of flowers. It was hard for her to tear herself away. She knew Ian would be amused when she let him know how she felt now, especially after having told him earlier on in their relationship that she was not keen on babies. She would have some explaining to do.

That evening, after they had eaten, she had the perfect opportunity to reveal her change of heart. She was sitting in their front room with her feet resting on the coffee table, admiring her selection of photographs in their individual antique silver frames. They had only recently been unpacked and placed on a small table bought for precisely that purpose. It had taken her ages to get them just as she wanted. There had been much tweaking of positions and shifting of angles before she had achieved the right look for each frame and declared herself satisfied with the end result. Ian was on the floor having a tussle with Millie and her bone.

"So what d'you reckon about Jane?" she asked. "She must have been delighted with her results. Gaynor and Mike must be pleased, too. She's done very well."

"I didn't manage to see Jane in the end and Mike was too busy being put out about her career plans to be pleased, which is a shame because she has done well. I tried to talk to him, but as predicted he was determined to be negative about everything. I'll have another go tomorrow. What was the baby like? I remembered to tell Gaynor."

"Oh good. He is absolutely adorable. I take back everything I said about babies a few months ago."

"What's that supposed to mean?"

Pippa giggled. "It means that I've been thinking and perhaps next year we might try for one ourselves."

"Oh really?" Ian said, a glint in his eye.

"I said next year, not right now. I've got to get some energy back first."

"Perhaps you should go and see the doctor, SweetP. You shouldn't still be feeling tired."

"I know. I've decided to see how I am in a couple of weeks and if I still feel out of sorts then, I will go. I promise. Let's forget that for now. I was just wondering as I sat here, when they might be coming to start the conservatory. Have they given you another date yet?"

"Should be the week after next with a bit of luck. All this rain has put all the schedules back."

Pippa stifled a yawn. "So we might have it ready for the August bank holiday, then?"

"Probably."

"You don't sound very sure. I'm only asking because I wanted to fit in a family barbeque before the summer's over."

"Not much of a summer so far, is it? Yes, I'm sure we'll have it done by then, don't worry. That's it Millie, go and lie down now," he said, giving the little dog one last pat on her head. Millie understood from his tone of voice that the fun was over and she trotted off to her basket carrying the bone proudly aloft.

Ian heaved himself up onto the settee beside Pippa. "I've had another think about cars," he said. He turned to face her, but Pippa had gone to sleep. She looked so peaceful sitting there that he decided not to wake her. "Never mind," he said quietly. "It'll keep."

12

Ian's optimism had been ill-founded. The weather did not improve. In the end it was well into September before the building work was finished and any barbeque they might have hosted would have been drowned out.

As the weeks passed, Jane and Susie went on their holiday and returned the best of friends. Mike's plan had backfired and Jane's determination to follow her vocation was as strong as ever.

There was no news to speak of from Hardale, except that Isobel had asked Ian and Pippa several times what their plans for Christmas might be and she had been lobbying hard to get them to go up north for the festive season. Pippa's energy levels had recovered a little, but she still did not feel quite right and she had made no firm promises to her mother.

"The river's running," Ian said one Saturday afternoon as he poured Pippa a cup of tea in their new conservatory. They were so pleased with the way this had eventually turned out that Ian had, with a touch of irony, christened it the West Wing. It was hexagonal in shape and roomy enough for the two wicker armchairs and a two-seater settee which Edith's wedding present cheque had funded. There was also a small, glass-topped table set in a grained oak base and its two matching chairs, which Ian and Pippa used when they breakfasted out there. On mild days, they opened the French doors and treated themselves to *al fresco* lunches.

Pippa had drawn the line at getting an aspidistra, but they had chosen a couple of architectural plants with broad tapering leaves and brown knobbly stems, which gave the room a tropical feel. Suspended from the apex of the pseudo Victorian glass roof was an impressive chandelier, complete with candle-effect holders gripping the neat, candle-flame bulbs. The double-glazed windows had blinds which, being cunningly sandwiched between the two layers of glass, were kept dust free and easily manoeuvrable.

Pippa often sat in the West Wing. She could relax in there and stare up at the sky, day or night, rain or shine, which seemed to be a good stress reliever. The night sky was her favourite. She loved the clear nights bathed in moonlight when the diamond chips of stars winked and shimmered at each other across the broad expanse of inky blackness.

Blue skies with a few cotton wool clouds came second. It was then that she could watch the wind urging their amorphous shapes into magical castles or giant animals or even into the profile of an ancient mariner with magnificent curlicue locks.

That afternoon there was nothing much to catch her imagination. Just the bland greyness of a leaden sky. As she gazed up through the glass, her mind was working overtime. She was trying to fathom the cause of her lethargy and her sense of malaise. She had come to the conclusion that she could not put this down to post celebration blues any longer. There was something wrong with her and it was high time she did something about it.

Ian was carrying on regardless. "It's uncanny the way it disappears for months on end and then I'm constantly amazed at how it turns up again year after year, as if drawn by some mystical force. I couldn't understand it when I was a child. Mum always made a point of taking us to have a look at the river when it was in full flow. It was the same routine every year. I can still feel the excitement of it now," he said eagerly. "Watching it race along the river bed, pulling all the long grass and weeds with it, dragging them down from the sides and stretching them out in the water. Like mermaids' hair, Mum used to say. Mike and I would throw sticks into the water and watch them float away. Have you ever played Pooh sticks, SweetP?" He looked across at her and realised that she had not taken in one word of what he had been telling her. "Pippa? Did you hear me? Are you all right?"

"Sorry, what did you say?" she said, finally with him again.

"I said the Syme's back," he reiterated with boyish enthusiasm. "It's not very deep at the moment, but it's certainly moving. I saw it this morning up by the dump. It's quite early this year. It must be all that rain we've had over the summer."

"What summer? I expect that's what's wrong with me, not enough sun. Anyway, I've been thinking and I've decided to go and see the doctor. I've put up with all this for long enough. I've made up my mind. On Monday morning I'm going to make an appointment to see Isla Ford."

Ian was relieved she had finally decided to be pro-active. It hurt him to see her so lethargic, but he knew it was her call. All he could do was encourage and support. "Do you want me to come with you?"

"Thanks, but there's no point," Pippa said, "I'll probably be in and out in five minutes. I'm expecting a lecture about putting on too much weight and not eating enough fruit, or something." She had not told him everything. What had finally prompted her to seek medical advice were the strange stomach cramps she had been experiencing over the past few days. She needed to know as soon as possible how ill she was and what treatment would be necessary. She did not want to worry Ian too soon. She had decided to say nothing about her new symptoms until she had seen the doctor. She would explain everything to him after that.

The following day she rang the surgery and made an appointment for Tuesday afternoon. The day and time suited her. She knew James would be out of the office for the whole of the afternoon and she would only have to make her excuses to Beth.

The surgery was barely a five minute walk away from the auction rooms and so, on Tuesday afternoon, just before four o'clock, Pippa left work and set off on foot to visit Dr. Ford. The waiting room was, as ever, replete with a cross-section of humanity. Old men with wheezy chests and rheumy eyes coughing their alarming coughs; middle aged women with puff pastry faces and well-rounded figures, their capacious handbags clamped firmly to their knees; young mothers looking tired and over-burdened with babes in arms or inquisitive toddlers in tow.

There were sullen youths sporting gold earrings, baseball caps and spotless trainers, fidgeting uncomfortably in their seats. Young women in tight jeans and high-heeled boots, squeezed into their snug quilted jackets with fur-lined hoods. Some of the young people had brought a posse of their friends with them, seemingly unable to function alone without mobile phones attached to their ears. Pippa had heard the receptionist tell each one of them, in turn, to switch off their mobiles and put them away. Surreptitiously, she rummaged in her bag to check that she had turned hers off.

She noticed that the walls of the waiting room were still covered in the colourful photographs of exotic locations set in cheap plastic frames which had greeted visitors to the surgery for as long as she had been registered there. Their purpose, she had always presumed, was to take the patients' minds off their current difficulties and transport them to foreign climes while they waited their turn with the doctor.

In Pippa's case though, this ruse had not worked. She was still very much in Linchester and just looking at her watch for about the twentieth time and wondering how much longer she would have to sit there, when the inevitable big brother voice invaded the tense, hushed atmosphere of the waiting room. "Philippa Flynn, room five. Straight down the corridor," it drawled in nasal tones.

Pippa closed the magazine she had chosen at random from the pile heaped up on a shelf by the reception desk and dropped it onto the empty seat next to her. It might as well have been written in Chinese for all the notice she had taken of it. Picking up her bag from the floor where she had let it drop the minute she sat down, she took a deep breath and then walked down the corridor to meet her fate.

She had known Dr. Ford for about ten years and in all that time had only ever needed the odd course of antibiotics. They were of a similar age and met more or less as friends. Dr. Ford visited the auction rooms from time to time to ask Pippa's advice about her collection of Swedish glass and they found chatting with one another, easy.

"Hello Pippa. I haven't seen you for a while. I'm tempted to say, *how are you?* But I always think that's a silly question to ask anyone in a doctor's surgery. *What can I do for you?* That's better," she said smiling over her glasses. They magnified her eyes to such an extent that Pippa thought they made her look like an old barn owl blinking lazily into the bright sunlight, especially with her unruly shock of feathery blond hair, beak-like nose and insignificant thin-lipped mouth.

"Actually, I'm not sure how I am," Pippa said, trying not to see Dr. Ford's chair as a perch. "I got married in July and I haven't really felt right since then or even for quite a while before then actually, if I'm being truthful." She went on to explain about the range of baffling symptoms she had been experiencing.

Dr. Ford unfolded her blood pressure machine. "Ok," she said. "Let's check you out." She gave Pippa a thorough examination, while at the same time asking her endless probing questions and on one occasion donning the dreaded surgical gloves, which immediately led to a different sort of probing altogether.

While Pippa was re-arranging her clothing and regaining her dignity, she went over to her desk and tapped something into her computer. Pippa sat down quietly and waited for her to finish while she went through the possibilities in her head. Could it be bowel cancer? Ovarian cancer? She had read a lot about that in the press recently and her symptoms seemed to fit. Bloated stomach, nausea, tiredness. Tiredness. Now that could mean Leukaemia couldn't it?

Her mind was running riot, her eyes dark with apprehension. If only the doctor would say something. She steeled herself for the anticipated bad news and then, when the suspense finally proved too much for her, she asked anxiously, "Is my blood pressure all right?"

"Yes, it's fine. In fact everything is fine. You seem to be in excellent shape, actually."

Pippa could not believe her ears. Had the doctor gone mad? Surely she was not imagining her symptoms? She had to know more. "Then why do I feel so tired all the time? It's not like me at all. And what about my stomach pains? Is it because I'm a bit overweight?"

Dr. Ford swivelled round in her chair to face Pippa. "You're not ill," she said reassuringly. "You're about four months' pregnant."

Pregnant? That was the one condition she had *not* considered. Pippa was aghast. "No. I can't possibly be."

"There's no *can't* about it," Dr. Ford said, an amused expression on her face. "You most definitely are. Surely you suspected it?"

No, she had not. Not for a minute. She sat rooted to the chair. Isla Ford must be mistaken. It was too soon. It must be the wrong diagnosis. Pregnant? No way. She could not take it in.

Dr. Ford looked down her ready reckoner chart and added, "According to what you've told me, the baby should be due at the beginning of February. Now let's talk about scans and while I'm about it, do you want me to change your surname on the files?"

"I don't know. I'm still having trouble coming to terms with what you've just told me. I'm pregnant?"

Isla Ford laughed. "Pregnant and in tip top condition. As long as you eat well and don't try and do too much, everything should be fine. I'm going to give you some leaflets about nutrition."

"Thanks." She was pregnant. There was a child growing inside her. Of course she wanted the same name as her baby. "Sorry. Yes. I would like you to change my surname on the files. I still use Flynn at the auction rooms, but I think I'd like to have the same name as my baby everywhere else."

Her baby. She was going to be a mother. What a strange concept that was... and yet, she had to admit, not an unwelcome one. She left the surgery in a daze, clutching leaflets on nutrition, keeping healthy in pregnancy and with the date for her first hospital appointment written down on a piece of paper tucked into the back of her diary.

13

Pippa did not switch her mobile back on. She wanted time to get used to the news herself, savour it alone before she shared it. Apart from which she wanted to look into Ian's eyes as she said the word *baby*. She did not hurry back to work and as she dawdled along the pavement, she made very little effort to control the foolish grin which insisted on monopolising her face. Afterwards, she was unable to remember what she had done at work for the rest of that afternoon except that she had managed not to let slip any clues to Beth. She was somewhat preoccupied with cataloguing new items for the September sale and not keen on chatting when Pippa finally re-appeared in the office. "You all right?" she asked without looking up from her task.

"Fine. I just got a lecture on my diet."

Beth was quite happy with that perfunctory explanation. It was, after all, perfectly true.

Ian was eager to find out what had happened at the surgery and he had tried Pippa's mobile several times during the afternoon. In the end he had given up and sent her a text message instead, urging her to ring him as soon as possible. He waited in vain. He was hurrying off home to get her news in person, when he was collared by Mike who wanted to discuss Jane, yet again. It was nearly seven o'clock before his car pulled up in the drive of twenty-seven Blain Gardens.

Pippa was in the kitchen, her ears straining for the sound of his car. As soon as she heard it, she stopped all scrutiny of her stomach and waited for him to appear. "Hello you two," she said as Millie bounded into the kitchen with Ian following close behind.

"Sorry I'm so late," he said. "I've been trying to ring you. What happened at the doctor's?" She stood in front of him, positively glowing, which prompted him to add, "That doctor must be good, you look wonderful."

"Come and sit down, Ian. I've got something to tell you." She took his hand and led him into the West Wing. "The good news is that I'm not really ill."

He wondered what was coming next "Not really ill? What does that mean?"

"Nothing bad, but I'm not telling you until you sit down."

Millie picked up on the excitement in the atmosphere and her ears rotated like radar dishes as she looked up at Pippa and turned her head this way and that. Ian sat down on the first available chair. "Right. I'm sitting down, so tell me."

"You said I looked wonderful and I'm going to give you some wonderful news."

"Are you?"

"I am. We're going to have a baby."

Their eyes locked. He seemed unable to understand her words. "Say that again."

"I – am – pregnant," Pippa said pointedly and then she giggled. "Four months' pregnant actually."

"Are you sure?"

"I'm sure and I feel a lot better now. Isn't it fantastic? I don't have to worry about losing weight or giving up chocolate, or anything. I know it's a bit soon, but you don't mind do you?"

Ian was frowning, doing calculations in his head. He was thinking back four months to the weekend of his fortieth birthday and the trip in a hot air balloon they had been given as a gift by Mike and Gaynor. His brow cleared and his eyes sparkled. "After the balloon."

Pippa laughed, "I think you're right. Hot air balloons should carry a public health warning."

"Life really does begin at forty," he said. He stood up and kissed Pippa tenderly on the lips. Holding her face in his hands so that blue could merge into green, he added, "We'll make great parents, SweetP. I can't wait."

A short while later, as they relaxed together on the wicker two-seater, Ian had a thought. "You know what this means, don't you?"

"No. What?"

"It's blown the convertible idea out of the window. My new car will have to be a people carrier."

"It's only one baby, Ian, not quads," Pippa said with a giggle. "Anyway, you've been talking about changing your car almost since we first met and you still haven't done it. I'll believe it when I see it."

"I'm still considering my options," Ian said. "Now I've got different options to consider, which will put the whole process back to square one."

"Well I'm just glad I settled for a hatchback and four doors when I bought my Renault. I should have plenty of room for a baby and all the extra equipment I'll have to carry round. Who shall we tell first?"

"I think it should be your Mum, but I can't wait to tell Mike. It might make him change the record at last. Now he's blaming Fr. Philip for encouraging Jane. He is, but she went to him, not the other way round. He'll be saying next that it was all Fr. Philip's idea. What rubbish."

"I'm sure he won't. He'll get used to the idea in the end. Ok, I'll ring Mum and Dad. Or we could both make a call at the same time," Pippa said. Now she had cheated death, she was feeling light-hearted. "I've already decided what I want to call the baby, Ian. At least it's what I want to call the baby if it's a girl."

Ian smiled. His Pippa had been restored to him. "Come on then, what is it?" he asked.

"Phoebe.

"That's nice. I like that. What if it's a boy?"

"I don't know. Somehow I'm sure it's a girl. We should have a biblical name too. You've got one and so has Mike. I've always felt a bit short-changed that my parents only gave me one name. What about, Ruth?"

"Fine, but we don't have to decide this minute, do we? Ring your parents," Ian said, laughing at Pippa's high spirits and feeling pretty good himself.

Isobel was watching a hospital melodrama when the telephone rang and Adrian was struggling with a crossword. "I'll go," he said, stuck on a devilishly complicated anagram.

"Hi, Dad. It's me."

"This is a nice surprise. How are you, Pippa?"

"Fine, thanks. Is Mum there?"

"She is. I'll just take the phone through." Adrian made his way back into the lounge and handed Isobel the telephone. "Pippa," he said.

"Hello, darling. Have you made up your mind about Christmas yet?" Isobel asked, thinking to herself how young all the doctors on the television looked.

"No, but I want to talk to you about something else."

"Yes? What is it?" Isobel had just caught sight of a gory operation on the screen and she was wondering how the producers managed to make it all look so real.

"I'm pregnant."

"You're what?" she said absent-mindedly as the patient expired on the operating table.

"I'm pregnant. Pregnant, Mum, hello-o-o." Pippa was put out that her mother was not reacting as expected.

Isobel blinked hard, swallowed and gripped the receiver. "Pregnant?" she asked in disbelief. Adrian put down his pen and looked at his wife.

"Yes, four months' pregnant. The baby's due in February. So much for seasickness. It obviously wasn't that at all."

"Pregnant," she said again. This was definitely not in the script. Isobel's eyes glassed over.

Adrian took the phone out of her hand. "What are you trying to say, sweetie? Who's pregnant? Mum's had a glass of sherry and she's away with the pixies, I'm afraid."

"I was telling her that I'm four months' pregnant. Quite a surprise isn't it? I only found out this afternoon. Ian and I are delighted, but ..." and Pippa's voice trailed off as she realised that her father wasn't listening either. She heard him saying, "Isobel, we're going to be grandparents, isn't that marvellous?" and then all she could hear was her mother sobbing, which was quite disconcerting.

"Pippa, are you still there?"

"Yes. What's up with Mum?"

"Overcome with emotion, sweetie. It's marvellous news. Well done. I'll get Mum to give you a ring tomorrow." Adrian put the phone down and turned to look at his wife.

"Isobel. What *is* your problem? I don't understand. You've always wanted to be a grandmother."

"I know and it is lovely for Pippa," Isobel said between sobs. "But I don't feel old enough now."

"Well, there's nothing you can do about that, is there? It's probably the shock. I'll make you some coffee. I quite like the idea, actually. What do they say? All the benefits with none of the responsibility."

"Mike's not in," Gaynor said when Ian finally got through to Migay Lodge.

He was prepared to be magnanimous. "You'll do," he said. "I've got some good news. Pippa's pregnant."

"Is she?" Gaynor said in surprise. "That was quick."

"Quicker than you think. The baby's due in February."

"Oh. Well. Good. We won't have so long to wait and she's got over the dicey stage without having to worry. I'm really pleased for you. Mike will be pleased, too. I'll get him to ring you when he comes in. Congratulations."

Pippa rang her grandmother next and got a much more positive reaction from her, but after they had finished chatting, Edith felt quite sad. Thinking of babies took her back to her own pregnancies.

There had been a baby before Isobel but she had died while still quite small and Isobel had never known her big sister. Although that had not stopped her asking countless questions about her, as children do. She had wanted to know where the baby had gone and Edith had told her patiently, time after time, that God had taken her to be one of his angels.

Isobel, quite as precocious as her own daughter was destined to be, had told her mother that God was selfish. He had plenty of angels already. Hadn't she seen them in the big picture Bible at her grandmother's house and in books at Sunday school? There were even more depicted in the stained glass windows of Hardale Church and what about the cherubs cavorting on the gloriously embroidered altar frontal?

Isobel had spent what seemed like hours staring at these smiling angels with their chubby pink cheeks and gilded wings and had made up endless stories about them while the vicar had droned on and on with his uplifting words that went right over a child's head. She had often wondered how many other babies had been purloined for this purpose. Yes, she had told her mother, God had an army of angels but Isobel had no-one to play with at home and it didn't seem fair.

Edith smiled at these recollections and wondered, idly, if her daughter remembered those conversations too. It was, of course, splendid news for Ian and Pippa and she had said so, but it had also made her sad that Ralph was not alive to share in her joy.

Her late husband had been creeping into her subconscious more than usual over the past few months. The disconcerting dreams she had experienced earlier on in the summer had ceased to trouble her but that strange visitation, if visitation was the right word, that had occurred in Hardale Church at Pippa's wedding, was still in the back of her mind. She had been left with the uneasy feeling that he had been trying to tell her something important and struggle as she might, she could find no way to discover what that was.

14

Pippa went into work the following day, a sense of excitement propelling her forward faster than usual. She left her car in the yard at McFarlanes and practically ran into the office. The improvement in her health since her visit to Isla Ford was amazing. Her energy levels had returned to normal and she felt ready to tackle anything. She realised that she had let her mind rule her health. It was her dire imaginings that had dragged her down and not some incurable disease.

She wondered what James would say about her news. She knew Beth would be pleased. At the very least they should both be surprised. She was smiling as she opened the office door. "Morning, Beth."

Beth was pressing different keys on her computer keyboard and frowning at the uncooperative screen. She only glanced briefly at Pippa as she came in. "Morning."

"Guess what?"

Beth was feeling stressed and not in the mood for frivolity. "What? I don't know. I'm not playing games. The computer's messing me about."

Pippa was not prepared to be put down. She wanted to milk her announcement for all it was worth. "It's not a game, it's stupendous news," she said.

Beth's eyes seemed to be glued to the computer screen. "Yes? If I have to read *Your file cannot be accessed*, again, I'll go mad."

Pippa persevered. "You'll want to hear this, Beth," she said. "I'm going to have a baby."

That did it. Beth looked up from her benighted computer. "What?"

"Pregnant. I'm pregnant."

"Fantastic," Beth said and then she added, shrewdly, "So that's why you went to see the doctor yesterday. So much for the lecture on food."

"Yes. All right. I did tell you a little white lie, but nutrition has a lot to do with a healthy pregnancy you know. What you should eat; what not to eat or drink and so on. Anyway the baby's due in February."

"February? Oh," Beth said, working out dates in her head, "I see."

Pippa was irrepressible. She giggled. "I'm saying nothing. Where's James?"

"Out. He won't be back until this afternoon, I'm afraid. Shall we have a coffee to celebrate?"

"I'd rather not," Pippa said, a look of distaste distorting her smile. "I've gone right off coffee. Tea would be lovely, though."

Mike had not returned Ian's call the previous evening because his meeting at the football club had gone on later than anticipated and then Mike, Dave and the captain had gone out for a few beers. By the time he finally returned home, Gaynor was fast asleep. It was breakfast time before he learned about Pippa's interesting condition.

"Pregnant? They didn't waste any time, did they?"

"The baby's due in the spring," Gaynor said not wanting to get into a discussion about dates and hoping that Mike would not work it out for himself.

Mike, though, was wide awake. "Spring? Mmm. That would be February, March time."

"February, actually."

"The sly dog. I wonder if it had anything to do with his birthday?"

"Mike, for heaven's sake. Don't you think it's good news?"

"Yes, of course I do, but you don't think he's going to escape some ribbing on the site do you? Oh bother."

"Now what?"

"This will mean more time off work, I suppose. He's only just come back from his honeymoon and now he'll want paternity leave. This Labour government's got a lot to answer for. How am I supposed to run a business with people trotting off on leave at the drop of a hat?"

"You had two weeks off when Jane and Susie were born. I think you've forgotten how tiring it is looking after a small baby. Ian loves babies; he'll want to do his share. Don't spoil it for him."

"Yes," Mike agreed after a moment's thought, "You're right, I had forgotten. I am pleased though, Gaye. It will be good to have another Chisholm to carry on the family name. It's bound to be a boy."

"Why is it?"

"Well, by the law of averages. We had two girls, so Ian's bound to have two boys."

Gaynor laughed out loud at her husband's reasoning. "You are funny, Mike. I don't think it works quite like that. As long as the baby's healthy and Pippa's all right, that's all we can ask."

Up in Hardale, Isobel had got over her shock at becoming a grandmother and she was upstairs, searching for something she had put away in a box somewhere. The box was nowhere to be found and she was getting impatient. "Adrian. Darling. Have you any idea where it might be?" she called.

Adrian was lying low in the garden and although the bedroom windows were open and he could hear his wife calling him quite clearly, he had developed a convenient case of temporary deafness. Then he had a better idea and started up the lawn mower. That would do it. He would not be able to hear anything above the noise that made. The dogs did not like the lawn mower. Nip in particular had an hysterical aversion to it. She started howling piteously. That started off Tuck who yapped in unison, which made Isobel come running down the stairs to settle them.

She picked up both dogs and, putting one under each arm, she carried them into the studio with her, shutting the door on all the noise. She put them down on the floor and then reached across the messy work table to turn on her ancient radio so that she could find some music to blot out the mower noise and soothe them.

Once peace had been restored, she started to think about her box again. Where on earth had it gone? Nip and Tuck were prowling around the studio, sniffing all the tins of paint and discarded canvases carelessly stacked up on the floor and then Tuck spied an old bone under Isobel's even older easel. She headed straight for it, knocking the easel over but revealing the box, which was sitting, waiting to be found, neatly propping up some books on the shelf behind it.

"You are *such* a clever dog," Isobel said picking up the easel and pulling out the box. She pushed some brushes and a wad of paper to one side and set it down carefully on her work table. "Now then, girls. Do you want to see what I've got here?"

When Adrian came back into the house a short while later, he found a serene Isobel making them both a cup of tea. "I found the box, or at least Tuck did. It was on a shelf in the Pod." She poured out the tea and then went to fetch her treasure to show him. "Do you remember these?" Isobel was holding up a pair of white kid shoes, scarcely more than doll-size, and an old silver teething rattle, which was not a pretty sight. It had obviously brought relief to more than one set of sore gums and was now tarnished and dented with age.

"Yes, I do. You haven't still got Little Moll in there have you?"

"I have," Isobel said producing a small rag doll with woollen hair and only one eye. "And I've got Tiger Tom too." She held up a knitted cat. It had orange and white stripes, string whiskers and two large, black, felt eyes. "Tim loved that old cat, didn't he? I was just wondering if I should parcel them up and send them to Pippa. It might make amends for me being so idiotic last night. Then I can ring her and tell her to expect a package."

"That's a very good idea, Isobel. If you wrap them quickly, we might just catch the post office before it closes for lunch."

Adrian and Isobel were keen to use their local post office as much as possible. It had, like countless others all around the country, been under imminent threat of closure. It was only there to be used because they, along with Edith, all their neighbours and sundry others, had successfully petitioned against its closure. They had even involved the local radio station in their campaign.

Eventually, after writing their letters, finding so many good reasons as to why it should stay open, attending so many protest meetings and persuading their Member of Parliament to lobby for them, the powers that be at the Post Office had relented. Against everyone's expectations, people power had triumphed and their vital amenity had been saved.

In Hardale, the post office was combined with a well-stocked general store. Theirs was a thriving village and they wanted it to stay that way. It was a magnet for visitors throughout the summer. They spent a small fortune at the village shop on souvenirs to take home with them, not to mention the postcards, picnic lunches, drinks and ice-creams they added to their baskets. The residents of Hardale had feared that if the post office left the village, then so too would their convenience store. They needed to be self-sufficient. In winter, when the roads in and out of the village often became impassable, the village store was a lifeline.

"I'll do it at once and then we can go down to the village with the dogs. They deserve an extra walk for helping me out," Isobel said. She drained her teacup and went in search of a stout box and some brown paper. Nip and Tuck had heard the word *walk* and their ears were standing to attention. Their terrier tails wagged with pleasure at the thought of some extra exercise.

Edith was also walking into the village. She wanted to buy some wool. In her experience, small babies needed hats and bootees. Pippa's baby would be born on the cusp of winter and spring and would need several of each. She thought it odd that cold feet should be an affliction of the very young and the very old and seldom bother anyone in between. Her own bed socks were worth their weight in gold to her. She did not do much knitting nowadays as her hands were so stiff and painful, but she was determined to make Pippa's little one something, whatever the cost to her joints.

Back in Linchester, the news of Ian and Pippa's baby had spread like wildfire. Ian had told Ivy, who had told the vicar, who had told his wife who was now safely back at the vicarage, who had informed her hairdresser, who had told Beth's mother, who had told her cousin, Skipper George. The Skipper had made Ian and Pippa's wedding cake and she was delighted to hear the news. She wondered if a christening cake would be next. She made a mental note to ask Beth when the baby was due.

Ian had also told Garth and Chrissie, who, coincidentally had been invited round for supper that Thursday night and they were the first ones to bring a gift for the baby.

"I couldn't resist this one," Chrissie said, giving Ian a soft honey-coloured teddy bear with marmalade eyes. "It's got a lovely squashy nose."

Ian took the bear from her. "Mmm. It's lovely, except that Mike would tell you that the bow's the wrong colour," he said, fingering the red satin bow round its neck.

"Oh yes. Linchester Wanderers are blue and white aren't they?" Garth said. "I shouldn't worry about it, Chrissie. Ian's not a fan. He's just winding you up."

"That's all right then," Chrissie said. "I wasn't bothered in the first place. I know what you two are like. You don't mind, do you, Pippa? You're not superstitious or anything?"

"No, not a bit," Pippa said. "I can't afford to be. After all, I'm the one who didn't even know she was pregnant. I thought I was sea-sick instead. It's lovely, Chrissie. Baby's first teddy. Thank you both. I can't say I'll put it in the nursery, because we don't have one, but I will when we do."

"Have you done anything about your new car, Ian? I suppose the convertible is out of the question now," Garth said. "You'll need something more practical. A people carrier or something."

"What is this fixation with people carriers?" Pippa asked. "I've already told Ian this. I haven't got a football team in here you know," she said patting her stomach, "It's only one teensy weensy baby. Your twins didn't stop you getting your Porsche, Garth."

"She's got you there," Ian said with a grin. He had spent endless pleasant hours discussing cars with his friend and the second-hand Porsche nine eleven Garth had finally bought, was his pride and joy.

Garth smiled. "That's because Chrissie already had a people carrier," he said.

"Trust me to pull the short straw," Chrissie said. She didn't look too unhappy about it. "Although, I'm not complaining because you can get loads of shopping in the back of my car and there's plenty of room in it for transporting children and all their rubbish. I end up with twice everyone else's amazing art works. The boys always seem to choose the biggest cereal packets and metres more bubble wrap then any of the others to make their space-ships or whatever."

"They're just expressing themselves," Garth said with a laugh. "We could have a pair of budding Andy Warhols."

"That reminds me," Ian said. "Could you help me with a little job, Garth? It's something I want to get down from the loft and I don't want Pippa lifting heavy things in her condition."

"Sure thing. It's a good job the boys aren't with us or they would be up there in a flash looking for ghosts or monsters or something and trying to 'help'. We'd never get them down again. They're dinosaur mad at the moment and into monsters in a big way. They find our attic fascinating. I don't know why."

"Perhaps they think there might be some strange creatures up there."

"It's empty, apart from their cot and a few old boxes."

"It's probably because it's dark and mysterious," Pippa said. "Sounds as if they've both got great imaginations. I hope you're not going to wrap me in cotton wool now, Ian. I've spent four months not knowing I was pregnant and nothing awful has happened, so I'd just like to be treated as normal ... with a bit of extra attention of course," she added with a giggle.

"You couldn't have helped anyway, SweetP. This is men's work," Ian said and then he beat a hasty retreat before she could answer him back. The real reason for him not asking Pippa to help was her fear of spiders. He did not think neat fear would be good for the baby.

The item in question was the rocking horse which was still stabled in the attic. Everything else up there had been cleared out and the horse remained in splendid isolation because it was such an awkward shape and Ian could not work out how to get it down on his own. He thought that, with him up in the attic and Garth underneath the hatch, they might manage it between them. The rocking horse, he thought, would look good in the non-existent nursery alongside the little bear.

Isobel's parcel arrived on Friday morning while Ian and Pippa were at work. Ivy took it in for them. She had something to give them, too. She had pushed a note through their door to let them know that the parcel was safe with her and it was Ian who called round after work to collect it. "Thanks for taking it in, Mrs. E. It saved us a trip to the sorting office."

"It's a pleasure, love. And this is from me. Just a little something for the baby. You can never have enough of these." She handed him a paper bag full of bibs with days of the week printed on them in bright colours.

"Thanks very much," Ian said. "I'd better get painting the spare room so that we've got somewhere to put all this stuff. The pile is slowly growing."

"Are you excited? I know it was a long time ago, but I can still remember how excited I was when I fell for Claire. I would have liked more children, but in those days they didn't know as much as they do now. There were no test tube babies then, you know. If you didn't get pregnant, that was it. Anyway, I was lucky because I only had one baby, but she was healthy and everything went well. I'm sure Pippa will be the same."

"The doctor says she's fine."

"Do you know what it's going to be? We didn't have any of these scans either and you never knew whether it would be a boy or a girl. Claire knew she was having a boy before Carl was born. She asked the girl doing the scan to tell her but I told her not to tell me. I didn't want to know. Carl was my first grandchild and as it turns out, my only one. It didn't seem right to know in advance. Are you going to ask?"

"I don't think so. Pippa hasn't had a scan yet. We're going to the hospital next week. I don't want to know whether it's a boy or a girl until it's born, either. Pippa's sure it's a girl for some reason, but it could be twin boys like Garth and Chrissie. You never know. Well, thanks again for this, Mrs. E," Ian said, waving the parcel in the air as he went back home to deliver it.

The only person who had slight reservations about Ian and Pippa's baby was James McFarlane. He had been planning to offer Pippa a partnership in the business. He had got to the stage in his working life when he thought it would be good to have a bit more spare time and he was trying to reduce his hours at the sale rooms. Pippa was the obvious choice for promotion. Now she was having a baby, he did not even know if she would be prepared to carry on working, never mind accept increased responsibility and, perhaps, longer hours.

He had discussed this dilemma with his wife and Hannah had advised sounding out Pippa before committing himself. She pointed out to him that a career and a baby were not mutually exclusive. It was entirely possible Pippa would want to continue at McFarlanes and everything could still work out as he had planned. So, after a weekend of geeing up by his wife, James arrived at the sale rooms on Monday morning ready to find out exactly where he stood. Pippa was helping Beth with some filing. "Would you come through when you've finished what you're doing? I want to discus something with you," he said. "And bring a coffee, would you?"

"I can come right away. We're done here."

"Good, good."

"I'll bring you both a coffee, when I've put this lot away," Beth said, helpfully.

Pippa smiled at her. "Not for me, thanks. Remember?"

"Oops," Beth said. "One coffee and one tea, then."

James took up his usual position behind his rather grand leather-topped antique partners' desk and waited for Pippa to sit down, too. "How are you, Pippa?"

"Very well, thanks."

"Excellent. I was wondering if, circumstances being as they are, you were planning to carry on working?"

"I was intending to, yes. At the moment I'm feeling fine and there's no reason why not. I think I'd go stir crazy if I had to stay at home all day."

"And when the baby arrives?"

"Well, I haven't had time to consider that yet, but I'd like to think that between us, Ian and I could juggle work and a baby."

"Good. In that case, I have a proposition to put to you. How would you like to become a partner in McFarlane & Sons? I've decided I'd like to back-peddle a bit. You don't have to give me an answer straight away, but don't leave it too long because I need to make contingency plans if you decide not to. An agreement in principle will do. We can discuss terms later."

Pippa's face lit up. "A partner? Thank you, James. I certainly will give it some serious thought." It was what she had been working towards. She loved her work and the buzz she got from auction days, tiring though they were. It would be an ambition realised if she accepted. It would mean she would have more responsibility and possibly have to work longer hours and now the baby was on the way, she knew there was no way she could manage everything without Ian's help. "I'd like to discuss it with Ian before I give you my answer."

James smiled at her. "I would have expected nothing less. It doesn't have to be tomorrow. Take a few days to decide. It's a big decision and you want it to be the right one."

Pippa left the auction rooms in high spirits. How lucky could she be? In the last year she had managed to find the love of her life, have a fairy-tale wedding, be expecting a baby and now she had been offered the partnership she had always wanted. Life simply could not get any better.

There was no sign of Ian when she arrived home but Millie was sitting at the bottom of the stairs looking soulful, which gave her a clue as to his whereabouts. "Ian, where are you? I've got news," she called out as she walked towards the little dog. "Good girl, Millie. Is he upstairs?"

Millie wagged her tail and gave a little yap in reply, which in turn prompted Ian to appear. "I'm up here," he said, his head hanging over the landing banister. "I'm just trying to work out how much paint I'll need." He had been as good as his word to Ivy and he was in the process of transforming their spare room into a nursery.

"I've been trying to ring you all day. Is there something wrong with your phone?"

"Battery's gone again. Sorry. Was it something important?"

"Yes, as it happens. James has finally offered me a partnership." He could see she was excited. "We need to talk about it."

He raced down the stairs two at a time and joined her in the hall. "That's fantastic, SweetP," he said giving her a hug. "You've waited a long time for this, haven't you? I hope you're going to accept."

"Of course I'd *like* to accept, but apart from the money side of it, can I manage a baby and more responsibility?"

"You're the only one who can answer that. If it helps, I'm happy for you to do it and I'm sure we could work something out when the baby arrives. Go for it."

Pippa hugged her husband back, her eyes shining. "You're one in a million," she said.

"I know," Ian said with a grin. "Actually, possibly one in ten million. The dinner's already in the oven."

15

As the non-existent dog days of that summer turned into the crisp mornings of early autumn, the inevitable build-up to Christmas took hold of every adult's inner child. Plans were being made, preparations under way and secrets and surprises hovered in the air. Jane was hoping for an early Christmas present. She was awaiting the interview Fr. Philip had arranged for her with the Director of Ordinands for the beginning of November. If he gave her the go-ahead, it would be her best early Christmas present ever.

She was showing a steely determination in relation to her chosen career. She had resisted all her father's attempts to get her to change her mind and she had read all of Fr. Philip's books. She had attended St. Jude's regularly since Ian and Pippa's wedding and, gradually, she had been persuaded to help with the thriving youth club.

Fr. Philip had been watching his young protégée and had come to the conclusion that she was a capable young woman with all the intelligence, compassion and humour necessary to qualify her to be put forward as a candidate for ordination. His only reservation was her lack of self-confidence. He felt sure, however, that this would diminish as her maturity grew. He hoped the Director of Ordinands would agree with his assessment and rubber stamp her serious training for the priesthood to begin the following year.

In the meantime, he had urged Jane to find a job to fill in her spare time so that she could gain some life experience outside the university campus. This was proving problematic. Jane could not find a suitable position and Mike, who might have been able to help her with this, was being deliberately obstructive. It was with this dilemma in mind that she went to visit Ian and Pippa one Saturday morning in late October.

Ian was busy putting the finishing touches to the nursery and Pippa had just returned from a walk with Millie. She was remonstrating with the little dog over her muddy feet when the doorbell rang. She was feeling in particularly high spirits. The anomaly scan and a blood test recommended by Dr. Ford to check that all was well with the baby, had not flagged up any abnormalities and Pippa had been assured that if her blood pressure stayed down, the rest of her pregnancy should be straightforward.

She hooked her wax jacket over the newel post at the bottom of the stairs and went to open the door. "Jane. Hi. Come in. This is a nice surprise. How are things?"

"Not bad," Jane said, stepping over the threshold and slipping off her duffel coat. "Except that I still haven't found a job."

"Oh no. Hasn't your Dad got any bright ideas?"

"No. He doesn't seem to want to help. Mum's had a few ideas, but they've come to nothing and I've lost count of the number of application forms I've filled in. All I've managed so far is a bit of bar work, which I hate. I was wondering if you could help? Can I smell paint? I thought you'd finished all your refurbs."

"Ian's painting the nursery," Pippa said, taking Jane's coat and suspending it by its hood over the top of hers. Suddenly, she stopped in her tracks, a startled expression on her face.

Jane looked concerned. "Are you alright, Pippa?"

"I'm not sure," she said, clutching the front of her grey cashmere sweater. "I just felt a very strange sensation in my stomach."

"Shall I call Uncle Ian?"

Pippa smiled. "No need," she said. "It's all right. I think I know what it was. I think the baby just kicked me. I've felt it before, but when it happened last time, I put it down to too much lemonade and broccoli. We haven't had broccoli since last week and I ran out of lemonade yesterday, so I know it's not that this time. It's unnerving knowing there's something, or at least some*one*, moving around inside you."

Jane was fascinated. "It must be weird. I can't imagine it," she said.

"It's gone now. It's like … like wind in the wrong place, I suppose. If it happens again, I'll tell you. It is a bit weird, but wonderful at the same time," Pippa said and then she giggled. She put an arm round Jane's shoulders. "Let's go and make a cup of tea and see if we can sort out this problem of yours."

Ian appeared on the stairs as they walked towards the kitchen. "Who's got a problem?" He was wearing an old blue-checked shirt with some rather shabby jeans and a pair of old trainers, a paintbrush balanced on a tin of pale yellow paint in his hand. Pippa's heart turned over when she saw him, his blue eyes crinkling at the edges as he smiled at his niece.

She had always thought that he and Jane looked rather alike, especially as Jane had very short dark hair and they both had identical sapphire blue eyes. It crossed her mind that her baby could be a miniature version of either one of them and then she wondered if it might have her auburn hair and green eyes. She was still privately convinced that the baby was a girl but Ian had insisted they refer to it as 'Junior' in case it was a boy and she gave him a complex. He had failed to persuade her, however and while she did always refer to the baby as Junior when talking with other people, just to please him, in her mind she was still Phoebe.

"Won't we, SweetP?" Ian said, bringing her back into focus.

"Won't we what?"

"You didn't hear a word of that, did you? She keeps doing this, you know, Jane. Just switching off, in a little world of her own. I think the baby's turned her brain to mush. Try and concentrate, Pippa, please," he said with a grin.

"Junior just kicked me. Did Jane tell you? It felt decidedly odd. I don't know about my brain, but it's certainly turning my stomach into mush and that's for sure. You still love me though, don't you?" Pippa asked with another of her giggles and she was rewarded with a heartfelt, "More than you know."

"Good. *Now* will you tell me what we won't do?"

"I give up," Ian said, shrugging his shoulders at Jane. "See what I have to put up with? I said we'd try and find Jane a job."

"Oh, is that all, I've already told her that," Pippa said. "Come on. Let's make that tea. I think we'll have it in the West Wing as the sun's shining."

In the end it was neither Ian, nor Pippa who solved Jane's problem. It was Tim. He was having a civilised lunch with his sister one dull day in early December because Pippa needed to discuss his Christmas arrangements with him. She and Ian had decided to drive up to Hardale. With the baby coming they could not guarantee when another visit might be possible and as her maternal hormones were running riot, she wanted to be sure that Tim would not be left all on his own in

Linchester over the festive season. She was hoping to persuade him to join the rest of the family up north for the holiday period and she was going to suggest that they travel up to Hardale together.

Tim was not prepared to make a snap decision. "I can't say what I'm doing, yet," he said.

Pippa changed the subject. "Ok. So what are your plans with the band?"

"I'm not sure my music career is going anywhere," Tim said. "I don't have the time to practice any more. Dave's getting married and Stu has decided to work abroad, so that just leaves Will. I think *Nimbus* is going to fold."

"Oh no. That would be a pity. Did you sell many copies of your CD?"

"A fair few, but you need to keep in the public eye to succeed. You know, performing live. Now my secretary has gone off trekking for six months, I'm snowed under, keeping my files in order and I wouldn't have the time to practice with the band, even if we were all still together. I'm having to work weekends to keep my head above water. It would help if I didn't have to do so much court work. You'd be amazed at how much time I waste hanging around, waiting for judges."

Pippa was listening carefully. "Ah," she said. "I may have a plan to help you. What do you need? Someone to answer the phone and take messages when you're not in the office? Do some filing, perhaps? That sort of thing?"

"Yes, more or less. You're not volunteering are you?"

"Of course not. Oh, I forgot to tell you. You're now talking to an almost partner of McFarlane & Sons. A bit more respect if you don't mind."

"Amazing. When did that happen?"

"Only recently. It's not finalised yet, we're still discussing the financial implications."

"You're not giving up work when you've had the baby, then?"

"No. Ian thinks we can manage between us, so I've accepted James's offer. It's what I've always wanted and I love it in the sale rooms, as you know. We've still got to work out the figures, like I said, but it should be sorted by April. That will give me enough time to get over the birth and work out some sort of a routine."

"So how are you going to help me out?"

"It's Jane. She needs a job while she's waiting for her training to start. She hasn't been accepted as a trainee ordinand for next year, but she's determined to be up to scratch for the year after and she needs something to do in the meantime. She's been doing a bit of bar work, but she doesn't like that much. She's a clever girl. I'm sure she could help you out. I'll give you her phone number."

"It sounds like an answer to prayer," Tim said.

"It's certainly an answer to Jane's prayer. Now let's talk about Christmas again. Are you coming up to Mum and Dad's with us, or not?"

But Tim would not be harried. "I've told you. I haven't decided yet. You make your own arrangements. I'll let Mum know what I'm doing in a week or so."

As Pippa had explained to Tim, the Director of Ordinands had made his decision. His view had been that Jane needed more time before she dedicated herself to training for the priesthood. Or, as he had so colourfully put it, she needed to *climb a few more branches of the living tree.*

It was a shame he did not think her mature enough but she took heart from the fact that he had not rejected her application out of hand. He had allocated her an adviser to show her the way forward and to guide her steps along the way and he too, had suggested that in the meantime she find herself a job, as well as continuing to help Fr. Philip with parish matters. Added to that, he had suggested that she shadow the hospital chaplain at St. Peter's, as and when she could, which would give her a much broader view of her chosen career.

Naturally, Jane was unhappy at his decision but he had promised to review her case after twelve months. She had to be content with that and set her mind to gaining some life experience. She was determined to fit the right criteria eventually and to pack in as much as she could into the intervening months.

Mike was as pleased at this turn of events as Jane was disappointed. He took it as a vindication of his stance on the matter. "This is excellent, Gaye," he had said to his wife on hearing the news. "Perhaps she'll see sense now."

Gaynor had frowned at him. "I do hope you're not going to tell her that. She's really disappointed."

"No, no. Of course not. I'm not stupid. I know. I'll pay for her to have some driving lessons. That'll cheer her up. And," he had added magnanimously, "If she passes first time, I'll buy her a little car, too. How's that?"

"Much better, dear, but do be careful what you say when you tell her."

Jane had accepted her father's offer with good grace. She had thought it an excellent idea. After all, she reckoned she would make a much better parish priest with her own transport. She did not, however, take the trouble to share this thought with him. Instead, knowing his volatile nature, she had taken his money and booked herself some driving lessons straight away in case he changed his mind.

16

Now that she had got over her second trimester, Pippa's pregnancy suited her. Her hair was thick and shiny, her skin glowed and apart from not being able to tolerate coffee, her appetite was healthy and her energy levels, good. The evening after her meeting with Tim, she was opening the post which had arrived while she was at work and discovered yet another letter from her mother.

After her lukewarm reaction to her daughter's pregnancy, Isobel had kept in almost daily contact with Pippa and regularly passed on little snippets of advice, as well as posting her relevant newspaper cuttings.

"I've had another one," Pippa said as she waved the letter at Ian. "I think Mum should take out shares in the Post Office. I'm sure she thinks now they've saved the one at Hardale, she has to use it every day, in case the powers that be change their minds again." She scanned the contents of her mother's latest missive and sighed. "Honestly, if it's not enough to wade your way through the minefield of contradictory evidence on food, apparently now it's exercise. I don't know where Mum finds all these articles. She must read every newspaper or magazine going. I bet she's not doing much painting."

Ian was getting ready to go out for a run with Millie and felt moved to support his mother in law. "She's an artist, SweetP. She can only paint if she's inspired." He grinned at Pippa. "It's not like a nine to five job, is it? Nice of her to bother at all. I quite like seeing what sort of suggestions she comes up with. Let's have a look." He walked over to read the article for himself. He had already devoured numerous books on pregnancy. He was fascinated by all the theories expounded by health gurus the world over, but had the sense to form no fixed opinions. He took his lead from Pippa. "I like this bit; it recommends swimming in the later stages. I haven't been swimming for ages. I think we should go. Or," he said, his eyes lighting up, "Perhaps we should buy you an exercise ball."

Pippa frowned. "Not a good idea," she said, firmly. "I got more scraped knees from trying to balance on my space hopper when I was little, than anything else. I don't think I'd be any good trying to balance on an exercise ball, now I'm so large. I'm up for a few swimming sessions though." She glanced down at her extra girth, a doubtful expression on her face. "Provided I can find a swimsuit big enough."

"I'm sure you will, you look fine to me. Let's go this weekend."

"Only if Alice can lend me something to wear. I'm finishing early tomorrow and she's coming over for a cup of tea. I can ask her then. All I've got are some skimpy bikinis, which would not be a pretty sight on me, especially with my boobs the size they are." Pippa giggled at the thought of it.

"Oh, I don't know," Ian said, ever the gentleman but not quite being able to ignore the vision in his mind's eye of his wife in her pregnant state, all skimpy bikini and vibrant auburn hair. He blinked determinedly and the vision disappeared. "I'm off for my run. Come on, Millie."

Alice and Pippa had met up a fair few times since Pippa's news had broken. They were never short of a topic for conversation and Alice, like Isobel, regularly shared some baby care tips with her. It was no surprise, therefore, that when she arrived the following afternoon, she brought with her some interesting information. "It's good news this time," she said, heaving her growing bundle from one arm to the other. "Chocolate."

"What do you mean, *chocolate*?"

"I've heard that a daily bar of chocolate is good for pregnant women."

"How come? I would have thought it would make you pile on the pounds even more."

"Well apparently it's all the theobromine it contains. *Theobromine*, I love that word don't you? It guards against pre-eclampsia and as you know, that can be a killer."

"Yes. Thanks, Alice. My blood pressure is fine at the moment and Ian and I are going to take up swimming, so I think I'll be Ok, but just to please you I'll make sure I eat more chocolate too. Have you got a cozzy I could borrow? I've only got bikinis and they definitely won't do."

Alice pulled a face at the picture this conjured up. "Not a happy thought, Pippa. Yes, I have. I've got a couple, actually. I'll drop them in tomorrow."

Oliver hiccupped dramatically at this point and started to grizzle.

"It's time for his feed. All right my little man, tea's on its way," Alice said, soothingly. She rooted about in her bag and produced a bottle of milk wrapped mummy-like in a muslin nappy. "Would you heat this up for me?"

Pippa took the bottle. "I thought you were breast feeding?"

"I was, but I gave up. He's always so hungry. He seems fine on the bottle and it makes everything much easier if I have to leave him with anyone. What are you planning to do?"

114

Pippa was already on her way to put the kettle on. "I'm going to give breast feeding a whirl," she called over her shoulder. "I'll have to see how it goes." Alice heard her giggle. "At least it will help save the planet if I manage it."

"What d'you mean?"

"I won't have to use plastic bottles or waste energy on heating up the milk, will I?"

As the holiday season approached, Pippa was beginning to get tired. She was looking forward to the Christmas break.

The days were disappearing, slowly but surely, under the wheels of the festive juggernaut. First, there had been the Chisholm Construction Christmas meal at a smart hotel near Arundel, complete with crackers and silly hats; hosted, of course, by Mike. He wore his special Christmas tie for the occasion.

His tie was not only special because of its outlandish depiction of Father Christmas sunbathing on a sandy beach without his hat on, but also because of its musical characteristics. When a concealed button was pressed, it played *Rudolph the Red-nosed Reindeer* several times over. This meant that each time he leaned across the table to speak to someone, he set it off. Gaynor, in desperation and much to everyone else's relief, finally insisted that he tuck the end of the tie behind his shirt buttons so that she could talk to the other guests without being interrupted by a musical interlude every five minutes.

Next, came James McFarlane's Seasonal Wassail and then a get together at Garth and Chrissie's had been swiftly followed by a mince pie and mulled wine evening at twenty-seven Blain Gardens. The grand finale had been a Carols by Candlelight service at St. Jude's.

Jane had urged and cajoled the youngsters of the parish to perform a half-decent rendition of *Little Donkey* at this service. In dressing gowns and the requisite tea towel headgear they were accompanied by a real live donkey, which had been drafted in for the occasion from the local donkey sanctuary. Oats, as he was known, was old and slow, but when he appeared through the west door at just the right moment, carrying a young Mary wrapped up in a blue velvet curtain, he produced a satisfyingly dramatic effect.

The whole Chisholm family were there to witness this spectacle and the fact that Jane had produced such a touching and meaningful performance made Gaynor glow with pride. Mike sat stony-faced throughout the whole service, but as everyone ignored his disapproving looks, they had very little effect, least of all on Jane. Earlier on in the evening she had received much praise and thanks from Fr. Philip for all her hard work and also, to her surprise, a colourful Christmas gift candle from her young charges, which touched her greatly.

Up in Hardale, plans were well in hand. They had also had a Carols by Candlelight service, albeit minus the donkey. The Christmas preparations were gathering pace. In the kitchen of The Old Schoolhouse, while Nip and Tuck slumbered in their basket, Isobel and Adrian were checking they had forgotten nothing. Isobel had a long list to hand.

"Have you ordered the turkey?" she asked her husband.

"Yes."

"Good. Have you bought all the wine and beer we need and some soft drinks for Pippa?"

"Yes."

"That's another tick then. When are you collecting the tree?"

"Tomorrow."

"What about the pudding?"

Adrian was finally goaded out of his monosyllabic utterances. "Oh no. You can't land that one on me Isobel. That's your mother's province," he protested.

"I just thought we should have a spare, in case. She's been behaving very oddly recently and I haven't dared to ask her if she's done it yet."

"She was fine when I called in with her shopping yesterday. I haven't noticed anything odd about her. I think she's worried about Pippa travelling all the way up here in her condition, that's all."

"She hasn't said anything to me about that. Anyway, there's nothing wrong with Pippa. She's been really well up till now and she's still got a couple of months to go. I expect Mum has been reading the tealeaves again and frightening herself."

Edith had not been reading the tealeaves, but she was worried about Pippa. The nearer the birth date loomed, the more worried she became. She had convinced herself that something would go wrong at the birth and try as she might, she could not shift her sense of foreboding.

If only she wasn't so old. What good was an old woman to anyone? She had not discussed her concerns with Isobel. She seemed confident that everything was going well. It was enough that one of them was a bag of nerves. The thing that irked her was that despite these fears of hers being completely irrational, she could not persuade herself out of them. Much as Edith loved Christmas, this year she could not wait for it to be over.

She wanted Pippa back home in Linchester and within easy reach of a hospital. Hardale was too remote should anything go wrong and if the roads became impassable? Well, that was just too awful to contemplate.

17

Despite Edith's worst fears, Christmas passed without mishap. It was over, almost before it had begun. Ian and Pippa had a safe journey. Eventually, Tim arrived but not until late on Christmas Eve and then he left again early on Boxing Day. The weather stayed fairly mild; not so much as speck of snow in the air, or a sliver of ice on the ground for the whole of the time the visitors from Linchester were in residence.

Ian and Pippa were both enjoying a week's holiday from work and they stayed in Hardale a few days longer than Tim. Edith gave herself a good talking to and ultimately succeeded in blocking out most of her worries, which meant that she managed, in the end, to have almost as much fun as everyone else. Nothing lasts for ever, though and when Ian and Pippa went home, her anxiety returned. She knew she would not rest easy until the baby had been delivered without mishap.

Pippa was now what her grandmother described as *bonny* and what Ian described as *a good armful*. She thought of herself as *blooming*. She was content to spend most of her evenings reclining on the sofa, dipping in and out of a bag of dolly mixtures, dressed in woolly socks, leggings, a selection of voluminous smock tops and a very long cardigan. Work was now a necessary inconvenience, but not for much longer, as Beth pointed out when the auction rooms opened up again after the Christmas break.

"You've only got a little while to go now," she said, moving out of the way as Pippa sailed in through the office door.

"Just two weeks until I finish work and then, well, who knows?"

"I thought the baby was due on the tenth of February?"

Pippa rested her folded arms on her well-rounded stomach. "Yes, but it could be early."

"That's just wishful thinking. Have you got everything ready?"

"I think so. The nursery's finished and the crib I bought here last month looks lovely in there. My bag's packed. I'm ready." Pippa sighed and sat down heavily behind her desk. "I'd be happy for the baby to come tomorrow. These last few weeks are such a drag. I sometimes wonder if my skin can stretch much more without giving way. I can't even reach my toenails you know. Ian had to do my nail polish for me last week."

"Did he? You've got him well trained. I don't bother with all that in the winter."

"I don't, usually, but everyone's going to see my feet in the delivery room."

Beth laughed. "You don't think they'll be looking at your feet, do you?"

"Probably not, but I felt I should make the effort. I don't want to let myself go just because I'm having a baby. Ian thinks I'm mad, but he's been ever so good about everything. He's going to make a great Dad."

"I'm sure he will. You'll be a great Mum, too. You haven't got long to wait."

"I hope not."

Junior must have been listening to this conversation. Pippa finished work in the middle of January and ten days later things started to happen. She developed a pain in her back, which lasted for a few days and made her right leg ache. Ivy told her the baby must be lying on her sciatic nerve and Pippa thought to herself that whatever nerve it was, it was unbelievably painful and made walking practically impossible. Then, early on the morning of the thirtieth of January, her waters broke and the contractions started in earnest.

She woke Ian at once. "It's started."

He sat up in a confused state. "What time is it?"

"About two o'clock."

"Shall I ring the hospital?"

"No. Not yet, I don't want to go in too soon. I'll wait until the contractions get more regular."

Pippa seemed to be in tune with her body and Ian felt surplus to requirements and a little anxious. "Shall I make you a cup of tea?" he asked. Paracetamol or a sticking plaster would not help but at least he could get her a drink.

"That would be lovely. Thanks, Ian."

Pippa's world had suddenly shrunk to the size of her womb. She was conscious of every little change in the atmosphere there, but of very little outside it. The slightest alteration to the status quo was immediately flagged up on her cerebral control panel. Finally, three hours later, the red light came on and stayed on. "I think you should ring the hospital, now," she said, calmly.

"What should I tell them?"

Pippa giggled. "Have you forgotten those ante-natal classes already? Just say my waters have broken, the contractions are coming regularly and that you're bringing me in."

"Right," he said. He could not believe how in control she was. He was having trouble making his arms and legs work.

It was barely half past seven when they arrived at St. Peter's. Pippa was seen straight away and settled into a bed. After that, events developed their own momentum and their baby emerged quietly into the world at ten past three that afternoon with very little fuss and bother and with only her father in attendance. The midwife had been called away for ten seconds at the crucial moment. Pippa had been right all along. Junior had become Phoebe Ruth.

Ian was overcome with emotion. "She's so cute," he said. "I can't believe how tiny she is."

Pippa laughed. "She didn't feel that tiny to me, but she is gorgeous."

"Yes. She's got a face like a cherub," Ian said, his voice no more than a whisper. "Hello, Phoebe." He found it difficult to take his eyes off the little wrinkled face. It kept blinking and grimacing, but there wasn't a sound.

"She's *our* little cherub," Pippa said.

"Isn't she quiet?"

"She's just getting used to being somewhere new. It must be quite scary for her. Hadn't you better go and make the phone calls?"

"Yes. In a minute." Ian stroked the palm of Phoebe's little hand and her warm fingers curled round his. Her eyes closed and she slept.

Mike and Gaynor were waiting for news, having been alerted by Ian at the start of everything. They were Phoebe's first visitors and they came laden with flowers and the most enormous teddy bear, three times the size of the baby. Mike's idea, naturally. Gaynor had favoured a cosy little white, all-in-one suit with pink, fluffy, bunny ears flopping out of the hood, but she had been overruled. She planned to go back for it the next day and give it to Phoebe as a welcome home present.

"She's beautiful," Gaynor said. "You tend to forget how small new born babies are. And she's got your hair, Pippa."

"Yes she has," said the proud father. "Did I tell you she weighed two point nine kilos?"

"No. That was a good weight. She seems very sleepy, bless her."

"I'm wide awake," Pippa said. "I don't feel too bad either and my stomach's nearly back to normal already. It must have been all the swimming we did."

"Well, I'm shattered," Ian said. "We've been up since two o'clock this morning. I'm sure I won't sleep tonight, though. I can't believe I'm a Dad. Awesome."

"You'd better believe it, mate," Mike said. "This is where all your money will go. Girls are very expensive." He issued his statement with feeling as he peered into the cot. "She looks much like ours did, Gaye. Although I think she's got quite a lot more hair than Susie."

"Yes. I love the funny little noises babies make, don't you Pippa? And they smell so sweet and irresistible. You just want to cuddle them all the time." A nurse walked past and glanced at her watch. "We'll have to go in a minute. All the other visitors have left," Gaynor said. "Come on, Mike."

They stood up to leave. "Try and get some sleep, mate. You're going to need it," Mike said as he gave Ian a gentle pat on his back. "See you when you get home."

Back at Migay Lodge, Gaynor rang her mother with the good news. "Pippa's had her baby. It's a little girl and she's absolutely gorgeous. We've just been in to see her."

"Aw, lovely," Gwynne said. She loved babies almost as much as her daughter did. "What have they called the little darling?"

"Phoebe Ruth."

"Lovely," she said again. "And how is Pippa?"

"She's delighted of course and not too tired. Ian's over the moon. I think he looks even happier than he did at their wedding."

"That's nice. I've got my little package ready. When do you want it?"

"I'm not sure. I expect Pippa will be home tomorrow. They don't keep them in long these days. I'll give her a few days to settle down and then we can both go round and visit the baby."

"Smashing. I can't wait to meet the little angel."

Shortly after Mike and Gaynor's visit, Pippa and the baby were moved into a private room, although they were not quite sure why. They weren't complaining. It was much more comfortable in there and nicer for them all to get to know each other away from the crying babies on the ward. It seemed the perfect start to family life. Their euphoria, however, was to be short-lived.

At nine o'clock that evening, everything started to unravel. Marcus Knight, Consultant Paediatrician, had only a bit part to play in the unfolding drama but it proved pivotal, nonetheless. He smiled pleasantly at them. "Do you mind if I examine the baby?"

Ian smiled back. He was holding Phoebe and thought it a reasonable request.

Pippa was not so accepting. Her maternal sixth sense had tuned into something in Mr. Knight's demeanour. "Why? There's nothing wrong is there?"

"I'd just like to examine her, to make sure," was all he would say.

The examination was a thorough one and Phoebe did not take kindly to being awoken from her slumbers, nor to having her blood taken, which upset her parents. What Mr. Knight was about to say next, upset them a great deal more. "Have you heard of Down's Syndrome?"

Pippa felt sick.

A chapter heading from the latest book he had been reading on child care, stood out in bold print in Ian's mind. *Children with Disabilities.*

"The results of the blood test will confirm it, but I am ninety-nine point nine per cent certain that your daughter has this condition. Do you know how it will affect her?"

They stared at each other in disbelief. They knew exactly how it would affect her ... and them. But there must be some sort of mistake. It could not be true. There had been no hint of anything abnormal about the baby throughout the pregnancy and Pippa had submitted herself to all the medical checks available. No, not their little Phoebe.

He took their lack of response as a lack of knowledge about the condition and he decided to talk them through it. "Her heart and lungs are sound," he said and then he went on to the flexible joints, poor muscle tone and how her learning abilities would be hampered by her slowness in processing information and learning new skills.

Ian looked at him blankly.

Pippa screwed up her eyes and screamed, silently, inside.

He wanted to finish on a positive note. "You won't have to cope alone," he said. "There's a vast support network in place for Down's children. I'll ask the social worker to come and see you. You'd be amazed at what can be achieved these days."

They felt alone at that moment, though. Alone and cheated. Someone or something had sneaked into their lives and snatched their adorable little Phoebe, replacing her with someone completely different.

"I'll come and see you again in the morning when you've had time to take it all in. I'm sure you'll have some questions for me by then and I'll be happy to answer them for you."

Having delivered his devastating blow, he left the room. They seemed such a nice couple and he had hated telling them. Distressing news was always difficult, but especially so when it involved a child.

"But I did everything right," Pippa wailed after he had gone, hot tears pouring down her cheeks. She had taken her hand off her life, looked away for a second and it had crashed. Impatiently, she wiped them away with the back of her hand while she looked at the tiny bundle, now fast asleep again beside her. "I never thought this would happen to me. Never. How on earth will we manage? How can we love this ... this changeling?"

Ian could not find the words. He gripped one of Pippa's hands and then she noticed that he too was weeping; silent tears. Pippa stroked his head with her other hand and sniffed pathetically. Finally he composed himself enough to say to her quietly, "Don't say that Pippa. She's part of you and me and we love each other. We can do it. I know we can. We'll find a way."

18

A few hours and many tears later, an exhausted Ian left the hospital and headed straight for his brother's house.

Gaynor answered the door and ushered him in. "Mike's outside with his fish," she said, wondering what had brought him round so early in the morning. "How's Pippa?"

Ian answered her abruptly "Fine." He walked outside to find Mike, leaving her to wonder what was going on. She had noticed his pale face and the dark shadows encircling his eyes. She had seen that look on his face before. It was just after his mother had died. Her heart sank. She wondered if something had happened to the baby but she realised that she would have to wait. Ian obviously wanted to talk to his brother alone.

Mike was checking that the fish were all right. The temperature had dropped dramatically in the night and he was more concerned about his carp than what Ian had to say. "What d'you mean she's got Down's syndrome? I saw her yesterday and she seemed perfectly fine to me. Ask for a second opinion. We don't have Down's syndrome in our family."

Ian looked unseeingly into the murky water. "They've done all the tests," he said in a hollow voice.

"I don't believe it and neither should you," Mike blustered. He bent over and peered into the depths of the pond himself. "Now, take my fish for example. The man at the pet shop thought they had fin rot and then when I looked it up in the internet ..." But Ian was not within earshot. He had walked over to the side gate and disappeared.

Mike stood up and straightened his back. "Ian," he called. "Mate?"

But there was only the distant sound of a revving engine. Ian had gone.

He was conscious of the fact that he could have handled things better. He considered running after him and then decided he was probably better left alone at the moment. Pippa would sort him out. It was then that another thought hit him like an electric shock. Ian would be bearing the burden completely alone. There would be no Pippa at home to comfort him. Pippa was still in hospital and would probably be in pieces herself … and then there was that poor little mite. Oh no. What had he done?

Mike walked slowly back into the house and headed for the office. He felt as if two icy hands had taken hold of his shoulders in a firm grip. For once he didn't even want to see Gaynor. He sat alone, locked in his office, his shoulders hunched over the desk. What sort of a brother was he? Ian had tried to confide in him and he had brushed him to one side. The least he could have done would have been to listen, for heaven's sake. He should have been able to deal with this. The truth was that he could not.

How could he ever look Ian in the face again? He had two healthy, normal girls. Ian did not have the luxury of normal. Mike thought he would never be able to look at the baby again either; that sweet little Phoebe who had seemed so like his own girls … and yet … not like them at all. The thought did not horrify him, that was not the reason. It was because Ian had been given such a burden to carry and Mike felt guilty.

The handle rattled as Gaynor tried to open the office door, bringing Mike's soul searching to an abrupt end.

He heard her voice, of course, but he did not reply. He could not.

"Mike? Mike. Open the door. What's happened? Where's Ian gone? He drove off like a mad man. Mike?"

Mike's body gave out a devastating sob and, unable to control his emotions any longer, he laid his head on his arms and bawled.

The news had by now permeated through to Hardale and Isobel and Adrian were just coming to terms with it. Adrian had promised Ian that he would let Edith know, to save him yet another call. He had reckoned that it was hard enough for him to explain everything once, never mind in duplicate. "Hello Edith." His voice wobbled and he had to clear his throat before he could carry on.

"Is that you, Adrian? You sound funny. Have you got a sore throat?"

"No. I'm all right. It's not me."

Edith knew instinctively that his news concerned her granddaughter. "It's Pippa isn't it?" She had been told about Phoebe's arrival and that despite her fears, everything seemed to have gone well at the birth. Although she had been relieved to hear it, her sense of foreboding still lurked beneath the surface. It bobbed back up again now with a tremendous splash. "Tell me at once. What is it?"

"It's not Pippa, it's Phoebe. She's got Down's syndrome."

Edith dropped the phone with a clatter. She could hear Adrian calling her name. Ever so slowly, she picked it up again. "It's all right, Adrian. I'm fine. I just need time to think. I'll ring you later."

Isobel was sitting in the kitchen nursing a stiff brandy. "I've told your mother," he said.

129

"That poor girl. I must go down and see her."

"We'll both go. Ian might need a bit of male company."

"What do you mean, darling? He's got Mike."

"I rest my case."

"Adrian."

"Look. I know he means well, but he's not a very sympathetic bloke. All I'm saying is that when you women get your heads together clucking over a baby, we men get pushed out. Don't forget I've had experience of this. Twice over. Ian's got issues to deal with over and above a new-born and he might need an ear that's not his brother's. I know it's not the end of the world and it could have been much worse. We've just got to hold on to that. Like Ian said on the phone, it's a blessing the baby hasn't got heart problems. Even so, he's probably got things he wants to talk about. I could listen, if nothing else. It might just help."

Isobel looked at her husband and smiled a watery smile. "That's very thoughtful of you, darling."

"Once we've all got over the shock we'll be able to see what's what. Edith took it badly. Perhaps you'd better ring her in an hour or so. Check she's all right."

Edith was all right. Much better than all right actually. She was busy packing a suitcase. Finally she understood. Her dreams made perfect sense to her at last. Better still, her sense of foreboding had left her completely. All was crystal clear. This was exactly what Ralph had meant. *The bairn needs you,* he had told her and Pippa did need her. All she needed was a lift down to Linchester.

Gaynor left Mike to himself for an hour and then she tried again. She tapped gently on the office door, armed with a mug of tea. "I've brought you some tea, Mike. Let me come in. Please?"

There was silence for a while and then Gaynor heard footsteps on the other side of the door. The key turned slowly in the lock and then the door opened to reveal a dishevelled and red-eyed Mike. "Something awful's happened, Gaye."

"Well, I gathered that. Sit down and drink your tea and then you can tell me all about it."

The storm had passed. Meek as a lamb, Mike walked back to the desk and returned to his chair. "How am I ever going to look him in the face again?"

Gaynor handed him the mug and kissed him on the top of his head. "It can't be that bad."

He took a sip of the hot, sweet liquid. "It's worse. He came to tell me something. I could see he was upset, but I didn't take enough notice. I brushed it off as if it didn't matter. It did matter, Gaye. It mattered a lot."

"What was it? What did Ian say?"

Mike looked at Gaynor, his face a picture of distress and then he sighed. "Phoebe's got Down's syndrome."

Gaynor let an involuntary, "Oh no," escape from her lips, which Mike latched on to straight away. "Precisely. I feel so guilty because there's nothing wrong with our two."

"Well that's ridiculous. There's no point feeling guilty. You know it's no-one's fault. It's just one of those things." Mike did not respond. Gaynor persevered. "It will be lovely to have a little one trotting round the place again. You must ring Ian and tell him you're sorry. Tell him we'll be there for him, that sort of thing."

"I can't."

"Do you want me to talk to him?"

"No."

"Well, we can't leave things as they are. He must be feeling really upset at the moment."

"I know that, but I'm upset too. I'd be no use to him. Let me calm down a bit and I'll think about it."

Gaynor knew she would get nowhere with Mike in this frame of mind, so she left him to his tea and went to phone her mother. "I've got more news about the baby."

"Oh yes? Are they back home now? When can we go round?" Gwynne said excitedly.

"It's not that, Mum. They're not home yet. The baby's got Down's syndrome."

There was a brief pause, during which she thought she heard her mother sigh and when Gwynne responded, her voice was much less animated. "Oh dear. What a shame. That must have been a shock. Pippa had all the tests didn't she?"

"Yes, but nothing showed up. Ian's in a state and Mike's even worse. Goodness knows what Pippa's feeling. I didn't mention this to Mike, but the baby might have other problems, too. What if she's got a bad heart or a weak chest? Thelma's boy had trouble with his heart and had to have an operation while he was still a baby. I don't know what to do, Mum."

"Have a word with Ian of course, or go and see Pippa again."

"Mike won't let me. He says he feels guilty because our two didn't have Down's."

Gwynne tutted to herself on the other end of the phone. "If you can't go round and see them, write

Pippa a note. Phoebe is still their new baby, whatever her problems are. All new Mums need a bit of extra love and support. What would you do if she didn't have Downs?"

This made a lot of sense to Gaynor and as soon as they'd finished talking, she went to find some writing paper and a pen. Mike might not know what was the right thing to do, but she did. She wanted to strike a cheerful note with her message and the blank, white writing paper seemed too stark. She searched a little further until she discovered a pretty greetings card down in the bottom of her stationery box. It was just an ordinary greetings card, blank inside, but the front was covered in a mass of bright spring flowers; perfect for the message of hope she was planning to write.

As she settled herself down at the dining room table with the card in front of her and a biro in her hand, Gaynor reflected that people were always too quick to label these children and then write them off. She knew from her years as a nursery nurse that Phoebe would have the same needs as any other baby and her own unique personality and talents. She would explain all of this to Pippa and then offer her love and support.

Isobel, Adrian and Edith set off for Linchester that very afternoon. Edith had phoned Ivy and asked if she could stay with her. She did not want to make a nuisance of herself at twenty-seven Blain Gardens. With her heart condition, she needed regular rests, which would not be possible with a new baby in the house. Ivy had agreed straight away. Ian had told her of Phoebe's arrival, but he had only informed Pippa's parents and Mike about Phoebe's condition, so it came as quite a shock when Edith told her the latest news.

"Poor little love. Well, they can always rely on me for baby-sitting. These days there's much more support out there than there used to be. I've read about it in the paper. I'm sure they'll find out that everyone wants to lend a hand. It's a shame Vera's not here. Ian could do with her help. She was a very understanding woman, Vera was and a practical one too. You would have liked Ian's Mum," Ivy said. She was thinking that she wished circumstances could have been different. Why had her friend had to die so soon? She hadn't been able to see Ian married; she hadn't lived to see his baby and now she wasn't here to give him the sort of support only a mother could give at such a difficult time. Ivy shook her head. She felt incredibly sad. "I'm glad you're coming," she said bleakly.

"I'm looking forward to the trip. Perhaps I can help, instead," Edith said, sensing her friend's distress.

Ian had told Pippa that her parents were coming to see her, but he was not aware of Edith's plans. Isobel and Adrian had not been able to contact Pippa direct. Her mobile phone had been switched off for a couple of days. She had not felt like speaking to anyone. She knew she could not stay incommunicado for ever and so, reluctantly the next day, she pressed the button that would re-connect her with the outside world. First, she checked her messages and it was not long before she was interrupted by a call from her mother. "We're in Linchester, sweetie. Can we come and see you later on?"

"Oh, Mum," Pippa said, her voice breaking. "It's so good to hear your voice."

"That's nice, darling," Isobel said. She kept her own emotions in check and carried on. "Gran's come down with us. She insisted. She says she wants to see you but she'd rather come on her own. I expect she thinks it will be too tiring with everyone else there. It can be difficult trying to get a word in edgeways when there are lots of people together in a small room."

"I don't mind. It doesn't matter whether you come as a job lot or not. I just want to see all of you. I need a hug," Pippa said pathetically. "Lots of hugs."

"We'll be over as soon as we can … and Pippa, the sun's still shining in the West Wing."

Pippa gazed aimlessly round her room after they had finished chatting. It was like a florist's shop. There were carnations, roses and freesias on every available space. Bursting forth from between spiky, long-leaved foliage or dark-green feathery fronds, they erupted enthusiastically from receptacles of every shape and size. She had received flowers from people she barely knew as well as from immediate family and friends and their combined perfume was impossible to ignore. There had been cards, too. Ian brought in another handful each time he visited.

She knew that her mother's cryptic comment was meant to remind her that life goes on in spite of everything and also to make her smile, but she did not feel much like smiling. She took in a deep, flowery, breath before she got out of bed and padded slowly round to the cot where Phoebe was lying, sleeping peacefully, oblivious to the emotional cyclone she had precipitated.

Such a good little baby, thought Pippa, sadly and then, falling back into the old habits of a happier and more hopeful time, she lent down over her daughter and spoke softly to her. "We're going to have some visitors soon, baby. Grandma's coming. And Grandpa. It's just you and me for now, though. I know we'll get through this somehow. My head's all over the place at the moment but I will love you, I promise. Just give me time."

19

Isobel and Adrian arrived at the hospital carrying even more flowers and presents for the baby. There were tears, but not many. The shock had passed and now it was time for more practical matters. Was Phoebe feeding properly? When was Pippa coming out of hospital? Did she have everything she needed at home?

Pippa had asked to stay in hospital for another day. She was not ready to face the world and when applied to, Marcus Knight had been sympathetic. He had agreed that Pippa and Phoebe could hide out at the hospital for one more day. Isobel and Adrian left, satisfied that everything that could be done had been done and promising to bring Edith over later. Pippa had just settled down for a rest and to torment herself with some more of the *How?* and *Why?* questions, when she heard a gentle knock at the door.

"Come in," she said without thinking.

It opened and standing in the doorway was a tall, thin, man, a clerical collar hanging loosely from his neck. He was somewhat older than Pippa. She noticed that as well as a closely-shaven head, he had strangely light, almost colourless, eyes but his smile was warm as it embraced her from across the room. She tried to smile back at him but her lips would not respond, the corners of her mouth locked in a down-turned position.

"I've been asked to come and see you," he said, his voice gentle, unintrusive. "I hope you don't mind." He stood on the threshold, waiting. "May I come in?"

Pippa was not in the mood to waste time on pleasantries. "Well, I'm not in the best of spirits, but I suppose it's all right."

He came into the room noiselessly, turning away from her briefly to check he had closed the door behind him. His pale eyes seemed to understand her anguish. "I'm Fr. Miles. Hospital Chaplain. I'm here to listen, if you want to talk." He sat down beside the bed, waiting for Pippa to give him a clue.

"We both know why you're here," she began, unwilling now, to look him in the eye. "But there's not much you can do to help." Her voice wavered. Somehow, she just managed to hold it together. She took a deep breath and started again. Her throat ached with the effort of controlling her tears. "You can't wave a magic wand and I can't turn back the clock, so I've just got to get on with it haven't I?"

He wanted to reassure her. "I know you won't believe this, but in a few weeks' time you'll be looking at things differently. The shock will have passed and you'll be feeling much more positive. These little ones have a way of winning you over. I've seen it happen; many times."

Pippa fiddled with her bedcover, her eyes still downcast. She could not accept what he was saying but she did not have the strength to argue with him. After a brief, awkward silence, there was another knock at the door and then a muffled but vaguely familiar voice that Pippa in her distraught state could not quite place.

"Excuse me; I'm looking for Fr. Miles."

"Do you mind?" asked the chaplain. Finally, Pippa raised her eyes to meet his. She shook her head.

"Come in," Fr. Miles called and the door opened.

Pippa was surprised to see Jane standing there. Jane was even more surprised to see Pippa. "Oh it's you. Oh dear. I'm so sorry, Pippa. I didn't know. No-one told me," she said, her face red with embarrassment.

"Do you two know each other?"

"Yes," Pippa said, every bit as unprepared as Jane. "Jane's my husband's niece."

"I'll go, if you would prefer to see Fr. Miles on his own," Jane said. She laughed nervously and shuffled her feet about in the doorway.

Pippa put on a brave face but still she could not quite manage to force out a smile. "No, I don't mind. You had to know some time anyway. Come in and sit down. There's another chair over in that corner."

Jane walked across to fetch the chair and peeped into Phoebe's cot on the way. The baby was stirring. "Could I ... I mean ... would you mind, if I picked her up?" she asked tentatively.

Pippa shrugged her shoulders, "If you want."

Jane reached into the cot and raised the baby slowly from her cocoon of blankets. "Hello, Phoebe," she said softly. "She's lovely, Pippa. My very first cousin, I'm so lucky."

Pippa said nothing. Jane was acting as if Phoebe was quite normal. She did not seem to be put off by the syndrome with which her daughter had been burdened. It did not seem to matter to her that she would never be like other children; other teenagers; other adults.

"Lucky?" she said eventually. "That's a funny word to use."

"Well, she is very sweet and I do feel lucky. Phoebe will always be very special."

This struck a chord with Pippa and the first link in the chain that would eventually bind mother and daughter together, was forged. Phoebe was very special. It would be a long haul but those words provided comfort. A small chink of light had appeared in Pippa's dark place.

"I don't think you need me," Fr. Miles said. The sound of his voice startled her. For a moment she had forgotten he was there. "I'll leave you in Jane's capable hands. Catch up with me later, Jane. I'll be around the hospital somewhere. Goodbye Mrs. Chisholm."

"Goodbye. Thank you for coming to see me. I do appreciate it."

"No problem. That's what I'm here for." He left the room as quietly as he had come, leaving a sense of calm in the room behind him.

"Well, here we are then, Jane. Not quite the happy family scene it might have been."

"I don't know. What I can see is a healthy mum and a beautiful baby." She hesitated slightly. "Erm, have you heard about Helen Keller, Pippa?"

Pippa wondered what she was getting at. She did not see the relevance of this random question and she could not care a fig about Helen Keller at that precise moment. Could this Helen Keller work miracles? Could Jane? On balance, Pippa thought not. She gave her a rather grumpy response. "I seem to remember something about her from school, but only vaguely. Wasn't she deaf or something?"

Jane was determined to get her point across. She ignored Pippa's tone of voice. "Yes, she was. Deaf and blind. She was an American woman who, after an illness as a baby, lost both her sight and her hearing."

Pippa wondered where this story was going. "Yes, that's right. I do remember, now. But I don't see what you're getting at."

"Well, eventually she triumphed over her disability. No-one thought she would. She became the first deaf and blind person to get a degree. Actually, that's not the point I'm trying to make. What I wanted to tell you is that she once said, when one door of happiness closes, another one opens. The only problem is that we're so busy concentrating on the closed door, that we don't even notice the one which has just been opened for us."

"Very profound," Pippa said. "I kind of see what she was getting at. My door seems to have been slammed shut, though, never mind closed … but thanks for sharing it."

The second link in the chain was forged later that afternoon when Edith finally arrived at the hospital. Isobel had left her at the entrance to the maternity ward and gone off to find them both a cup of tea. She asked the nurse in charge where she could find her granddaughter and appeared at Pippa's door a short while later.

Pippa was lying on her bed, staring into space. She was surrounded by cards and flowers. Edith's heart went out to her she looked so forlorn but her mission was enlightenment and never having been one to wallow in self-pity herself, she was determined that she would persuade her granddaughter out of hers. She tapped on the open door with her stick and spoke in a brisk, but kind tone. "Pippa, lovey. How are you?"

Pippa had not noticed the door opening. She had been too busy thinking her gloomy thoughts. On hearing her grandmother's voice, she looked up and managed a smile. She got up from her bed straight away and walked across to give her a hug. The kind words had left a constriction in her throat and she could not speak.

Gently, Edith persisted. "Well, how are you?"

Pippa swallowed hard. "Not good, Gran. Feeling a bit sorry for myself, actually."

"Yes, I see. I expected that. How is my great granddaughter?" she asked as she sat down on the regulation padded hospital chair.

"Doing well. I think that's the expression. Shall I bring her over to you?"

"Yes, please. I want to see her."

Pippa carried the sleeping baby over to her gran and Edith held her carefully, smiling down at the little bundle in her arms. As she did so, the years rolled back. "She's got those dear little ears ... and the eyebrows," she said, as if to herself.

Pippa did not understand. "What do you mean, Gran?"

"Sit down, Pippa. There's something I want to tell you." Edith waited while Pippa settled herself down on the bed again and then she began her story. "A long time ago, when I was even younger than you are now, barely more than a bairn myself, I had a baby."

"Yes," Pippa said. "My mother."

"No," Edith replied. "Not your mother." Pippa's eyes widened a little. She could not imagine what was coming next.

"Let me explain. At around the time of your wedding I wasn't sleeping very well. My nights were plagued with dreams about your grandfather that left me feeling uneasy for hours afterwards. Dreams are funny things, Pippa. They stalk you as you sleep and then haunt you when you wake. Your grandfather was on my mind the whole time. And then something strange happened. I shouldn't have been surprised after all that dreaming, but I was. I thought I saw him up at Hardale Church on your wedding day." Edith took a deep breath and sighed. "I heard him, too. He was telling me that you would need me. I didn't understand it then. It seemed like complete nonsense and I blamed it all on the new medication Dr. Lock had given me. Now I believe he *was* there and it wasn't nonsense at all. Now I do understand."

Edith looked across at Pippa to see if she was all right, but her granddaughter was resting on her bed, listening with rapt attention. She settled herself more comfortably in the chair with Phoebe in her arms and carried on. She was talking softly now, her Cumbrian lilt making the whole story seem more like some epic poem, her eyes fixed on the sleeping baby. "Our little baby, our first born, had Down's just like your Phoebe, although it wasn't called that then."

Pippa sat bolt upright. Her whole body portrayed her surprise. Her eyebrows soared as she gasped in astonishment. "Oh, Gran. No." Edith looked up for a moment and then carried on with barely a pause. "Our baby, unlike your Phoebe, had a bad heart. The doctors could do nothing about it and probably wouldn't have even if they could. Down's children in those days were hidden away from sight and considered freaks. Unforgivable. Our baby, though, she was precious. My mother insisted that I keep her with me for however long she had on this earth and she helped Ralph and me as much as she could. She looked upon the baby as a gift from God, just lent to us for a while because she needed special help."

Edith stopped to move Phoebe, who had begun to stir in her sleep and she looked up at her granddaughter. "Like you, to begin with I was upset. I wondered why it had happened to me; what I'd done to deserve it." She sighed and hesitated for a moment. "But the baby brought me so much happiness, I can't tell you. I know your Phoebe will do the same for you. You are lucky though, Pippa. Phoebe doesn't have a weak heart like my baby did. You're not going to lose her just when you've come to love her dearly."

Edith had said her piece and as she looked lovingly back down at Phoebe, she rocked her gently in her arms. Pippa felt the tears well up yet again, but this time she was not angry, or even sad. She felt ashamed. Ashamed that it had been all about her. She had not been thinking about Phoebe and her needs. Her grandmother had made her think about her baby as a person and not just as a syndrome. Pippa was ashamed that she had practically written off her daughter before she had even given her a chance. "I can't believe what you've just told me, Gran," she said when she felt ready to speak.

"I know it's a shock at first. It was to me," Edith said, sadly. "No-one knew much about the condition in those days and what's worse is that it's not what you are expecting. I had such dreams for her."

"Yes. I had dreams, too."

"Well, you'll have to have new ones now. I look at it like this," Edith said, not willing to let Pippa dwell on the negative. "It's only one little chromosome too much and what's that in the scheme of things? A mere bagatelle. I'm going to have to explain all of this to your mother now. She'll be here in a minute. She went to find us some tea. She only knows part of the story and I expect she'll be upset with me for not telling her. I'm not sure why I didn't say anything before. Perhaps it's taken me this long to get over it. What I am sure of, is that you and Ian are going to make really good parents. Just give yourselves a chance, lovey."

Pippa emitted a small, self-conscious cough and then she got off her bed and walked over to her grandmother's chair. "Thank you so much, Gran. I think I see it now.

It's odd, but Jane called in earlier and she said she felt lucky to be Phoebe's cousin and you think I'm lucky to be her mum and I'm just beginning to feel that way, a little bit, myself. I can't wait for Ian to come in again tonight so that I can explain it all to him. What did you call your baby?"

Edith smiled. "I thought you might ask me that," she said. "Well, she was my little Ruth."

20

"No-one told me about Phoebe," said an indignant Jane as she ate supper with her parents that evening. "I was shadowing Fr. Miles at the hospital today and her room was on our list but I didn't know who was in there. I was really surprised to see Pippa. I thought they'd been discharged. She seems very down about everything."

"She must be. Poor Pippa. Sorry. I was sure I'd left you a message. I'm not thinking straight at the moment. You weren't here when Ian called round and we haven't seen much of you over the last couple of days. You're always so busy. It was a bit of a shock for all of us. I'm waiting until she comes out of hospital and then I'm going round to see her," Gaynor said. "I want to tell her about Thelma's son. He has Down's and he's at college now, learning all about plants and gardening. He has quite a full life. Thelma told me the other day that he even goes out to the pub with his friends at the weekends. It's not all gloom and doom, you know."

Mike, who had been tucking into a bowl of creamy rice pudding, listened to this exchange without comment but as his wife finished speaking, he put his spoon down and scowled at her. "It's not right, though, is it? Why did Ian and Pippa have to be saddled with all of this? This is just the sort of thing you're going to have to deal with, Jane. Helping people to cope with what life throws at them. What is your God thinking of? Has he got a conscience? Why Ian and Pippa?" he asked again, his bitterness spilling over. "For heaven's sake, we've only just got him right after Mum dying. What's this going to do to him?"

Jane could see that her father was upset. Her voice was gentle as she answered him. "I don't think that's fair, Dad. Why not Ian and Pippa? Between them they are probably more able to give Phoebe a loving home, full of opportunities, than a lot of other people I know. Phoebe is a beautiful baby and from what Pippa said, she's physically fit. We're all going to have to support them and spend time with them to show them that we care about *all* of them."

Gaynor looked at Jane and saw her in a new light. She was growing up fast. Her compassion shone through and she wasn't scared of saying what she thought any more. These last few months of working with Fr. Philip and his colleagues had obviously taught her something. "I agree with Jane," she said. "You're going to have to talk to Ian again sooner or later. Shall I ring him up and ask him round for a chat?"

"No."

"Mike, he needs you. You are all he's got left. You can't just ignore him."

Mike suddenly stood up. He pushed his chair back from the table with such force that it left the neglected spoon jangling against the side of his bowl. "Didn't you hear me? I said, no," he shouted. He clenched his fists, a fierce expression on his face and then, shooting both his wife and his daughter an angry look, he left the room without uttering another word.

"Oh dear," Gaynor said.

"I think he's more upset than anybody else," Jane said. "You'll have to work on him, Mum. I just seem to make him worse."

"He feels guilty, Jane. He can't get over the fact that you and Susie are ok and Phoebe will never be the same as you. Ian will be all right, I'm sure of it. It's Dad we have to worry about."

Ian did not know whether he was all right or not. He knew that when he held his daughter in his arms he felt overwhelming love for her whatever her problems, but he was worried about Pippa. She seemed so negative and she seemed to have shut herself off from him and the baby. He was hoping that after she had seen her parents, she would begin to improve.

With Isobel and Adrian available to visit Pippa and look after Millie, Ian had started his day several miles away. His drawn face and hollow eyes had affected Edith greatly. She had taken him to one side and suggested that a breath of fresh air might help. Ian was reluctant, but Edith had called on Adrian for support and he had eventually agreed that they could do the day-time visiting and he would leave seeing his little family until the evening.

After breakfast, he drove down to the coast, parked his car in a deserted car park and walked briskly along the beach with the wind from the sea stinging his ears. It made his eyes smart and encouraged the tears that had been threatening, to roll down his cheeks. He let them fall, unchecked. There was no-one else about and he was too weary from maintaining a stoical attitude for Pippa's family, to care anyway.

Seagulls wheeled and soared overhead, their haunting cries stifled by the blustery wind that thwarted their progress across the sky. He noticed their frustrated efforts and empathised with them. He, too, was trying hard to make headway but his mind was all over the place, whipped up by a hurricane of emotions which impeded rational thought and blocked his path to peace and tranquillity.

He made himself trudge over the skittering pebbles as a penance. With his tears spent and in a renewed effort to cleanse his mind and eliminate his hopelessness, he stooped to pick up several of the smooth, round stones and then lob them into the roaring tide as hard and as far as he could. It swallowed them quickly. He picked up another handful and one after one, using his arm as a catapult, he fired them off into the foam. The physical exertion seemed to help and, for a while, he found some peace.

He drove back to Linchester in a better frame of mind, but as he neared the town, his despair returned. He wandered around, aimlessly. He sat down in his favourite Costa with a large Americano to hand and having sipped his way through that, he walked across to the Cathedral.

The organ was playing, softly. Vergers were going about their duties, footsteps muffled by their reverence. As he glanced from one side of the building to the other, he could see visitors wandering up and down. His ears caught their whispers as they marvelled at the windows and magnificent tombs. His mind finally let go and he found solace in that warm and hushed interior. Gradually, his inner strength returned. It came to him, kneeling there, his head in his hands, what he could say to help make things better for Pippa.

He would tell her that he needed both her and the baby home with him as soon as possible. He would tell her how much he loved them both. He wanted them to celebrate Phoebe's birth, not resent it.

On his way back to the car park, he took a shortcut through one of the many little passageways which formed a cat's cradle through the back streets of Linchester. He emerged at the far end of East Street. At the junction of the twitten and the main road was a dusty little shop full of other people's cast-offs. Antique jewellery; pieces of yellowing lace; ornate china vases. In the window, next to a monstrous black clock and a moth-eaten fur jacket, sat a rosewood box, banded in silver and with a silver cherub ornamenting the lid. It was small enough to find a place in anyone's home and big enough to be a useful receptacle for precious items.

He glanced at the window as he passed and the cherub gleamed at him. He stopped in his tracks. He thought the box might show Pippa how much he cared about her and that he was proud of their baby. He was certain she would like it. Hand hovering over the shop door handle, he was undecided. As he stood there, wavering, the door opened and a strong smell of air freshener greeted his nostrils. "Excuse me," said a sharp voice.

He was blocking the doorway. "Sorry." Ian stood to one side and allowed the young woman to leave.

She was clutching a cumbersome old chair with broken webbing on the seat and appeared harassed. "Going in?" She held the door open with her foot.

He nodded. "Can you manage that?"

"Yes. I only live round the corner. I'm always doing this. I go into a shop to browse and end up taking something home with me. It looks a bit sad, doesn't it? Can't leave it in this state. All it needs is a bit of t.l.c."

Of course it did and that was exactly what Pippa needed. The box was just the thing to help him explain. "Thank you," he said with feeling.

The girl was startled. "What for?"

"Oh nothing. Good luck with the chair."

The young woman shrugged and heaved the chair out of his way.

Ian made no further detours, but before he set off on his journey home, he switched on the radio hoping for some local news. A CD started to play instead. He recognised it straight away as one of Pippa's favourites. It was the track she had chosen to play a few months earlier when she had been altering the wording on their wedding invitations and then again on their way in to the hospital when Phoebe's arrival was imminent. That seemed like a life-time ago to him now. As the music played, something delayed him setting off. The words of the song spoke exclusively to him. The Feeling were serenading him with *Strange* and it went straight to his heart …

Everyone knows we're strange …

Everyone knows we're different, so why do you feel ashamed? We love you all the same …

Unencouraged, underrated and unappreciated …

We love you all the same.

Ian was definitely not ashamed. His little girl might seem strange to others as she grew up, but he loved her all the same and Mike's attitude, in particular, was stuck in the middle ages. He did not need it.

He squared his shoulders. He felt stronger now and more able to deal with his emotions and therefore more able to help Pippa with hers. He knew it was harsh, but unless his brother could be supportive and accept Phoebe for who she was, then he would have nothing more to do with him until he could.

21

Tim had a secret. He had told no-one. The reason he had made his trip up to Hardale at Christmas such a short one, was that he had met someone special and he had wanted to spend time with her, too, over the holiday period.

One day, a few months back, Jasmine Mears had appeared in his office, asking for advice about a divorce. This was not Tim's speciality and he had referred her on to one of his colleagues but their friendship had blossomed and although still in its infancy, it seemed so right that he felt he could now afford to share it with his family.

There was another reason why he had put off revealing his news. Jasmine had a son. Bryce was seven years old. He knew Ian and Pippa would not mind that, but he could not be too sure of his parents' reaction to him taking on a ready-made family and so he had waited until he was sure the relationship had a future, before he told them.

Pippa's news had been a shock to him and he could not even begin to imagine how she must feel about it, or what Ian's reaction might be. He felt sorry for them, but his desire for everyone to meet Jas and Bryce ultimately overrode any other consideration and he had decided that the time was right to reveal their relationship. He thought it might give everyone something new to talk about and dilute the impact of Phoebe's problems for a while. He reckoned that after Pippa and Phoebe were safely back home from the hospital and while his parents and grandmother were still in Linchester, would be the ideal time. He rang his mother to see if she agreed with him.

Isobel was back from the hospital and just sitting down with a cup of coffee when the phone rang. It made her jump. She was miles away, thinking over what her mother had just told her. She was delighted to hear Tim's voice. "This is a nice surprise," she said.

"How are things?"

"We're all at sixes and sevens, here. Gran's just told us something completely unbelievable."

"Has she? What's that?"

"It's about the sister I never knew. Where to start?" Isobel said and then, as quickly as she could, she explained all about Ruth.

Tim was as amazed by her revelation as everyone else. "I can't believe she kept it to herself for so many years."

"I know, but things were very different in those days. I suppose she had it drummed into her not to talk about it. We're hoping it will help Pippa to accept what's happened to her. She never told me the baby's name, either. Fancy Pippa and Ian picking the same one."

"That *is* weird."

"Sorry, Tim. Never mind me rambling on. I didn't think. Were you just ringing for a chat or did you want to tell me something important?"

"There was something. I... um... I've got someone I want you to meet. We've been going out together for a few months now. As you're staying down here for a bit, it seemed like a good opportunity to introduce you. Save us trailing all the way up to the Lakes."

"How lovely. Of course I want to meet her. What's her name?"

"Jas."

"Is that short for Jasmine?"

"Yes."

"Not Jasmine Little?" said Isobel, calling to mind an old nursery friend of Tim's.

"No. I think she's in London now. This is Jasmine Mears. There's something else, Mum."

"She's not married is she?" Isobel said, only half joking.

"Well, sort of. She's waiting for her decree absolute actually. It's not that. She's got a little boy. Bryce." Silence. Isobel took a deep breath. It would seem that it was one thing after another with her family, but her free spirit, was not going to be unsettled.

"Really? Well, bring him along, too."

"Would that be all right? You're sure you don't mind him coming?"

"No. It will be fun."

"Great. Thanks Mum. How's Pippa doing?"

"As you would expect," Isobel said. "Still coming to terms with everything. It was a tremendous shock for her and for Ian. For all of us, really."

"Yes. It's hard to know what to say. What's the baby like?"

"She's sweet. Just like any other new-born. She doesn't seem to cry much and she's very sleepy at the moment."

"I'm sure Pippa will feel better about everything once she's home again. Hospitals aren't very relaxing places, are they? Is there anything I can bring her?"

"Just yourself. I know she'll be pleased to see you."

Isobel said her goodbyes and went off to find Adrian. "It's the other one now."

"What do you mean?"

"Tim's been on the phone."

"Oh. What's he done? Not having a baby is he?"

"Actually, he might be."

"Isobel, please explain yourself."

So Isobel repeated what Tim had told her about his new relationship. "I'm a bit worried. Do you think she's a gold digger? She might just want someone to help bring up her son."

"You're very cynical, all of a sudden."

"Well, she has been married before and Tim hasn't had much luck with picking women, has he?" Isobel said. "There was that awful Kate, who wanted him to emigrate to Australia. Then we had Natalie who smothered him and now Jasmine and her complications. He's a nice catch for someone. He's good looking. He's got good prospects."

"We'll just have to trust him on this one. I'm reserving my judgment until I meet them," Adrian said. "You should have asked Ian before you agreed to them coming round here, you know. You'd better run the plan past him when he comes in. It is his house."

"I know that. Of course I will."

Isobel had a word with Ian as soon as he came back from his wanderings and he was happy with the arrangement. "I'll tell Pippa this evening. I don't suppose she'll mind. She'll want to see Tim. She should be back home tomorrow, which will give her time to settle in with the baby before the visitors arrive. I think I'll have a shower before I go back to the hospital."

He was just about to leave the room, when Isobel put a restraining hand on his arm. "Wait a minute,

Ian." She thought it would be wise for him to know the family secret before he saw Pippa that evening. "I've got something else to tell you."

He sat down again. "What's that?"

"Mum went in to see Pippa this afternoon as you know and dropped another bombshell on us."

"Should I be worried?"

"Not really. What she told Pippa might have helped her come to terms with everything. It was quite a story."

Ian was fascinated. "Go on then, tell me."

"Mum explained all about her first baby. There was another little girl, before me. Adrian and I knew that I had a sister once, of course. We all knew that, but what none of us knew was that she had Down's."

He was shocked. "What? She didn't tell anyone?"

"No. Well. I had always assumed that the baby had only survived for a few hours because of some complication at the birth. Mum never, ever went into details about her. I suppose because of the stigma around Down's children at the time. Now it turns out that the baby actually survived for a few months. She didn't live very long because she had a heart condition. Mum didn't even tell me her name. It was always *the baby*, or *your sister*, when I was growing up which is why I presumed she had died shortly after her birth. Eventually, as time went by, she was hardly mentioned and I had all but forgotten about her. Naturally, Mum hadn't."

Ian, although stunned at this news, was sympathetic. "No. You couldn't forget something like that," he said. Such secrets in such a close family. Perhaps this was just what Pippa needed. Someone who could empathise with her. "How did Pippa take that revelation?"

"Mum said she thought it had helped. That's not all, Ian. The baby did of course have a name."

"And?"

"The sister I never knew, was called, Ruth."

"No," said Ian. "Bizarre." He was thinking to himself that everything was in a state of flux. Whatever next? He wondered if they were about to find out that Ivy had a toy boy. Was Adrian running a gambling syndicate? Or perhaps they would discover that Tim was a criminal mastermind. He could not wait to visit Pippa now and see what she thought about all of this. His system had been re-balanced and he had regained his sense of humour. The trick was to pass on a small phial of his recovery to Pippa and get her to swallow it. It might take time, but he was now even more confident that he could nurse her back to full health.

He left for the hospital as soon as he had eaten the coq au vin and treacle tart that Isobel had prepared for him and found Pippa waiting impatiently for his visit. Phoebe had just settled herself into a good feeding routine. Although still a sleepy baby, she had learnt how to suckle and Pippa was beginning to enjoy breast feeding her. Her sensible head told her that breast feeding was best and she wanted Phoebe to have a good start in life. She owed her that much at least, after all her negative thoughts.

Ian was a little anxious as he entered Pippa's room. Was his hunch correct? Had her grandmother's visit helped? He had lost a little of his optimism on the drive over to the hospital and he was not quite so sure of the reaction he was going to get from her. He tried to smile as he approached the bed. "Hello, SweetP."

He need not have worried. Pippa had got over the shock. Even her feelings of self-pity were beginning to recede. She got out of her bed and gave him a big hug. He knew straight away that something had changed. He felt his face breaking into a broad grin.

"I've got such a lot to tell you, Ian."

"And I can't wait to hear it all, but before you start, I've got something to give you to show you just how much I love you and our baby," he said taking the little box from his coat pocket and giving it to her.

"More presents? You didn't have to. I know how much you love us already," she said as she removed the paper bag. "Oh Ian, thank you. It's so unusual. It's lovely." Pippa traced the cherub's chubby cheeks and then opened the lid to look inside. "What an unusual box. I love the little angel on the top. No, it's a cherub, isn't it?" Straight away she understood what he was trying to convey with his gift. "You are sweet, Ian. I'm very lucky to have you."

"I'm the lucky one," he said and kissed her cheek.

"Did you hear about Gran's announcement?" she asked, a twinkle in her eye.

He nodded. "Your family is astonishing."

"It's unreal, isn't it? I can't believe her name was, Ruth." That delicious giggle that had been so conspicuous by its absence over the past few days, suddenly escaped from her lips and he knew then for certain that her recovery had begun.

22

The next day, after all the formalities had been completed, Pippa and Phoebe were discharged from hospital. Pippa was uncharacteristically anxious. "I'm really nervous, Ian. It's all down to us, now."

"I'm sure your mum will want to help."

"I know, but Phoebe is so small. What if she doesn't stop crying?"

"I don't think we need to worry about that while your parents are still here and when they've all gone back up to Hardale, we can always ring Gaynor if we're worried. It'll be fine."

They arrived home to be greeted by a welcoming committee which included Edith and Ivy, both of whom had parcels for the baby, a multitude of comforting words, plus numerous hugs and kisses for them all.

"Where do you want to sit, Pippa?" Isobel asked. She was fussing over her daughter as if she were still a baby herself.

"The lounge, I think. Phoebe had a feed just before we left the hospital so she should sleep for ages now."

"Ivy's got a present for the baby," Edith said, as she installed herself on the seat next to her granddaughter.

"Has she? Thank you Ivy."

Ivy handed over her parcel. "You're very welcome."

It was a peculiar shape and wrapped in white paper with little pink rabbits playing leap-frog, printed all over it. Pippa quickly tore open the paper, while everyone else looked on.

"I thought it would go in the nursery for her to watch when she's lying in her cot," Ivy said. "Babies love colourful things."

Pippa untangled the component parts and made a discovery. "It's a mobile," she said. She held it up in the air for everyone to see. It was based on three criss-crossed plastic rods, suspended from which, by differing lengths of fine wire, were numerous butterflies and bees in a mixture of shades and sizes. Bright blues and greens; soft pinks and yellows; dotted, striped and plain. She held it up and blew at the butterflies, making them bounce into the bees and then spin off to turn freely in the air. The whole thing looked like some mad, dysfunctional kaleidoscope. "Look, Ian. Isn't it amazing?"

"It certainly is. Phoebe's going to love it. Thanks very much, Mrs. E. I could go and fix it up right now, if you like. Then it will be ready when she goes to bed."

"No. Wait a minute, Gran's got something for the baby and anyway I think she'd better sleep in with us for a couple of nights while she gets used to her new surroundings."

Isobel was horrified at the thought of Phoebe sharing their bed. "Not in your bed with you," she said. "You might roll over and squash her."

Pippa giggled, "No. Don't be silly, Mum. She'll be in her crib beside the bed."

Ian said nothing, his eyes alight with love for his wife. He could see that her dismay and disappointment had passed. She had nothing but positive thoughts now. They would be working together, doing their best for their daughter.

Edith's parcel was resting on her knees, wrapped in silver paper and with a big, pink, bow on the top. "D'you want this one, now?"

"Thanks, Gran. Ooh. It's really squashy. I wonder what it is?" Pippa undid the wrappings and gasped.

Despite finding it extremely difficult with her stiff fingers, Edith had made not only bootees and bonnets for Phoebe, but also the softest, prettiest shawl Pippa had ever seen. It was pure polar white, knitted in a pattern reminiscent of conjoined cobwebs. The shawl felt warm to the touch and was as light and fluffy as a melt-in-the-mouth meringue. It was quite beautiful in its fragile complexity.

"I love it, Gran. Thank you so much. I thought you weren't doing any more knitting."

"I don't knit as a rule, but Phoebe is my first great grandchild and I was determined to make her something special. I'm so glad you like it."

Pippa kissed her gran on both cheeks and handed the shawl over to Ian so that he could test out its softness as well. "It's beautiful, Edith," he said and passed it on to Isobel.

She cuddled it to her cheek. "Mmm. It feels as soft and warm as cashmere. I'd be happy to snuggle up to it, myself," she said. She passed the shawl over to Adrian. "Here, darling. You have a feel. It's almost like swansdown, isn't it?"

"Yes. Very nice," he said, giving the shawl a perfunctory squeeze and then he hung it carefully over the handle of Phoebe's new stroller.

"I'll go and make us some tea, shall I?" Isobel said. She disappeared off into the kitchen while Ivy and Edith chattered on and the tea arrived in due course, along with a plate of shortbread biscuits.

Edith noticed that Pippa had gone quiet. "You must be tired, lovey." She put her teacup down on the coffee table. "We'll go and let you have some peace," she said.

Ivy nodded enthusiastically as she rose from her seat. "That's right. Lots of rest. That's what you need now."

Isobel went to see them out and Ian collected all the pieces of the mobile into an unruly bundle. "I think I'd better go and fix this up before we lose all the bits and pieces," he said, heading for the door. "I noticed Millie eyeing it up earlier. I'd hate her to swallow one of those bees. We don't need a trip to the vet just at the moment."

Adrian, however, remained in the lounge with his daughter. "Well, you're home now, sweetie."

"Yes, I am. Thanks for staying on, Dad. Ian said you told him you could stay for another week."

"We'll stay for as long as you need us. The dogs are fine with Will Grace and I quite like being on my old stamping ground again. I've caught up with a few people and Millie and I have walked for miles. 'Solvitur ambulando'," he quoted.

"Which means?" asked his mystified daughter.

"A broad translation would be that you feel better after a good, long, walk. It works; solves most things, Pippa," said her father sagely. "Although I could have done without all the surprises we've had recently. I think I'm suffering from bombshell burn-out."

Pippa laughed, which was a surprise for both of them, but mostly for Pippa, herself. At one stage over the past few days she had wondered if she would ever laugh again. Her nightmare was slowly fading as she gradually came to acknowledge that it had not been much of a nightmare in the first place and anyway, she did not have to face the struggle alone. She had Ian by her side and her family behind her. "Gran's news was quite a bombshell, wasn't it?"

"She's a dark horse, your gran, but Mum took it well, I'm pleased to say."

"I'm looking forward to meeting Tim's new girlfriend, aren't you?"

"He's another dark horse. Hasn't been as snowed under with work as he'd have liked us to believe."

"No. I wonder what she's like?"

Her father was prepared to be upbeat. "Probably perfectly normal," he said and then he looked at Pippa with a serious expression on his face. "What I'd really like to know, Pippa, is how *you* are."

Pippa smiled at her father and then she sighed. "Well, I'm getting there. Yes, I think that just about sums it up."

23

Ian decided to go to church with Adrian on Sunday morning. Isobel was pleased. She wanted some time alone with Pippa and Phoebe. She had a scheme in mind and she needed to share it with her daughter. "I'd like to do something special with you before we go back home," she said as they sat together in the West Wing. "I thought a visit to Marble Hall might be just the thing."

"Marble Hall?" Pippa asked, "I don't think I've heard of it. What is it?"

"It's a holistic retreat near Horsham. Dad and I found it on the internet. I thought we could have a day out there. Just you and me. I'm sure, between them, Ian, Dad, Mum and Ivy can manage Phoebe. We could have a facial, a massage or even a detox and then treat ourselves to some lunch there, too. They do good organic food apparently. We could just relax for the day. Goodness knows you need it after what you've been through. The web page says they have treatments for the mind, body and soul and I thought it would set you up. You know, boost your energy levels."

"Mmm. It's a nice idea but I'm not sure. Can I tell you in a few days' time? I could do with a bit of pampering, but I don't know if I'm up to a whole day out just yet."

"That's fine. We'll probably have to book anyway. I'll ring up tomorrow and see how much notice they need. Right. Now I'm off to sort out lunch, but first I'm popping next door to see if Mum can make a cake for our visitors this afternoon. You stay there and put your feet up. Make the most of the peace and quiet."

Isobel was destined to be disappointed. Her mother had gone to church with Ivy and the friend who gave her a lift there each week. She was at that very moment listening to Fr. Philip's request for his congregation to think about their giving to the church. The organ was in dire need of replacement and he was hoping to drum up a bit of support for the fund-raising team. It was tiresome having to discuss finances again, but a parish could not be run on fresh air and he felt it would do his parishioners no harm to face up to that fact.

"If any of you would like to host a coffee morning," he said. "A car cleaning session, perhaps? Do a sponsored swim even, or anything else you can dream up that might help raise some funds for the organ fund, please let me know. We can put all the details in the parish newsletter. For those of you who just want to donate cash rather than time or talents, don't forget to put the money into one of the envelopes you will find at the back of the church. That way we can claim the tax back." He checked his notes. "I think that's all the notices for now. Thank you."

He returned to his seat and turned to face the congregation, arms uplifted. "May the road rise to meet you. May the wind be ever at your back. May the sun shine warm upon your face and the rain fall softly on your fields and until we meet again, may God hold you in the hollow of his hand." A minute after "Thanks be to God" rumbled round the church, the first few notes of the final hymn rang out.

At the back of the church, Adrian nudged Ian. "Remind me to pick up an envelope on the way out," he said. "I'm going to put some money in. Good church music deserves a decent organ. I liked the music at your blessing service. I know how hard it is to raise funds for a church. We had trouble with the roof up at Hardale and even with grants, it took years to get the money together."

"That's good of you," Ian said. "I shouldn't think Mike will be so generous." He smiled across at Gaynor and Jane who were sitting surrounded by the Sunday school children. "Mrs. E said she might hold an afternoon tea party in her garden in the summer. I think I'm going to do a sponsored run with Millie."

"She'll enjoy the exercise. My walks don't seem to tire her out at all. Cracking little dog. She doesn't yap either. I like that." Ian smiled as Adrian flipped through the pages of the hymn book to find the right number; he remembered Nip and Tuck's noisy welcome when he and Pippa had visited The Old Schoolhouse at Christmas and Adrian's exasperated efforts to silence them. "Sensible hymns at your church, too. Nothing comes close to a good Wesley."

While Pippa and her mother had been enjoying their cosy tête à tête at twenty-seven Blain Gardens and Fr. Philip had been shaking the begging bowl at St. Jude's, over in Symington, an unexpected visitor had arrived. Susie had decided to pay her parents a visit.

She was concerned at recent events in Linchester and, reading between the lines, she thought that her help might be needed. At times like these, she reckoned families should stick together and she had brought with her a secret weapon which she hoped, with the optimism of youth, would make her father see sense. She had told no-one of her trip, except for her grandparents and Lol Roberts had driven to the station to meet her.

The train arrived ahead of schedule and Susie was waiting on the pavement outside as his car slowed to a halt in the empty car park. "Hi Gramps," she called as she ran across and jumped into the passenger seat beside him, heaving her overburdened shoulder bag onto her knees.

"Cariad," he said. "The train must have been early for a change." They shared a satisfying hug together. "You're a good girl, you are. I know your Mam will be pleased to see you. Your da is like a bear with a sore head at the moment."

"I thought as much. Mum would never criticise him, but sometimes he's impossible. Anyway, I think I might be able to turn him round. We'll see."

Gaynor had not returned from church by the time they arrived at Migay Lodge. She liked to give Jane as much driving practice as possible and a trip to St. Jude's with a little detour on the way back, was an ideal opportunity. Being Sunday, there was very little traffic on the roads. They both wanted her to pass her driving test at the first attempt so that she could take advantage of her father's generous offer. The only person at home was Mike the Moody. He was incarcerated in his den pretending to do some work.

"It's very quiet in here," Lol said. "Where's your Da?"

"I expect he's in the office."

"I think I'll wait in here until your Mam comes home. Just in case," Lol said, as he opened the kitchen door.

"It'll be fine, Gramps. Don't worry about me. Dad's a pussy cat really. I'm not like Jane. I can give as good as I get."

She found her father sitting at his computer as she had expected, his back towards the door. She noticed that the screen was not covered in figures as it would have been had he been doing some serious work, but in his favourite tropical fish screensaver. He seemed to be staring, vacantly, out of the window, his mind obviously miles away. "Hello, Dad," she said.

Mike spun round in astonishment at the sound of her voice. His face broke into a smile. "Susie. What are you doing here?" He got up from his seat and accepted her daughterly embrace.

"I thought I'd come home and see what's been going on." She looked into his face and saw a sadness in his eyes that had not been there before. She squeezed his hand. "I also want to meet my new cousin. What's she like, Dad?"

Mike's face fell. "She's quite a nice little baby actually. A bit like you were, but with a lot more hair."

"And how's Uncle Ian?" she asked, knowing full well from a recent conversation with her mother that he had not seen his brother for several days.

Mike looked glum as he resumed his seat. "Don't know," he said.

"What? Haven't you been round there yet? I thought Pippa was home now." Susie was really jerking his strings.

"She is home but I can't go. I feel like a complete fool. I don't think I'll ever be able to look her in the face again, or Ian come to that. I'm scared to look at the baby after what I've said and thought. I've made a real mess of things haven't I?"

"Nothing that can't be sorted, Dad. I'm here to help you. It's Susie to the rescue," she said and with that, she tugged a huge sheaf of papers out of her shoulder bag and deposited them on the desk in front of him. "Da – dah," she cried as the papers thudded home. "I've been doing some research for you."

Mike looked at the untidy pile of paper before him, a bewildered expression on his face. His hands clung on to each other for support but remained resolutely immobile on the desk in front of him.

Susie adopted a severe tone. "Well? Surely you're going to see what I've brought for you?" He scanned the covering folder, but said nothing. He had registered that it was an information pack for new parents of Down's children. He looked up at her, a small pulse beating in his throat, his eyes blinking rapidly.

"Open the booklet," she ordered. "Read the first page. Key words you're looking for are shock, embarrassment and rejection." She waited for a few moments while he did this and then she added, "Now page three. Can you see the paragraph that says it's never anyone's fault?" Mike nodded unhappily. "It also says *don't feel guilty*. Have you got that, Dad?"

Mike nodded again and then he smiled. "This is quite interesting actually. I did look up Down's syndrome on Wikipedia, but it was a bit too technical for me. This is much easier to understand. D'you mind if I read the rest of it?"

"Of course not. Go ahead. That's exactly what I want you to do. While you're doing that, I'll grab myself something to eat and then we're going to discuss a telephone call you have to make."

Susie left the room in double quick time because she did not want to give her father a chance to argue with her and she also thought she had given him quite enough to think about for the moment. She wanted to give him the time to take it all in. Apart from which, she was hungry. She returned to the kitchen, where her grandfather was sitting waiting for her, his ears alert for any sign of raised voices.

"Phew, that's it then," she said as she flicked her blonde hair to one side and dramatically wiped the back of her hand across her forehead. "Or, as Nana would say, *all done and dusted.*"

"I didn't hear an explosion, so I take it your campaign was a success?"

"So far so good. I think I'm winning, but we'll have to wait and see." Susie plonked her empty bag down on the kitchen table. "Now, I wonder if there's anything good to eat in here?" she said as she headed for the fridge. "I'm absolutely starving."

When Gaynor and Jane returned to the house about an hour later, Susie had just gone back into the office, replete with cold pasta and chocolate cake. Lol was sipping a beer at the kitchen table.

Gaynor was surprised to see her father. "What brings you here?"

"Your whirlwind of a daughter," he said, his dark eyes gleaming up at her as he gave her a good-natured grin.

"Susie's here?" Jane asked.

"She certainly is. She's in phase two at the moment."

Gaynor was puzzled and beginning to feel uneasy. "Whatever do you mean, Dad?"

"She's having a go at Mike and good luck to her, I say. This stand off has gone on for long enough."

Jane punched the air with vigour. "Yes. Go Suze," she said.

"Oh dear," Gaynor said in a weak voice as she sank into the nearest available chair.

24

Later that afternoon as the sun had put in an appearance, everyone including Millie had assembled in the West Wing. She was curled up under Pippa's seat. The little dog had been her constant companion since her return from hospital and she found this rather touching. When Ian opened the front door to greet the visitors, Jasmine was the first to walk in, followed by Tim who was holding the hand of her little boy.

She was striking; tall, with straight, jet black, shoulder-length hair and faultless make-up. She was wearing a sheepskin jacket over a calf-length black skirt and knee-length black leather boots.

"You must be Jasmine. Welcome," Ian said. He smiled at her pleasantly. "We're all in the conservatory as the sun's shining."

She did not respond to his warmth. Her face was a mask. Removing her coat, she handed it over to him. "Thanks."

He noticed her perfectly manicured fingernails, the heavy, diamond-encrusted gold band on the third finger of her right hand and the ostentatious watch hand-cuffing her wrist. Her cream cashmere sweater was classic with its round neck and long-sleeves. It was encircled at the waist by a wide leather belt fastened with a silver buckle. His eyes were drawn to her left arm by the many and various gold bangles that jangled there as she smoothed down her hair. Everything about her screamed, *expensive*. She was certainly an attractive woman but she had a slightly superior air about her and Ian was not sure he liked what he saw. She had such cold grey eyes.

"This is my son." She pulled the reluctant child forward. "Come here and say hello, Bryce."

He turned his attention to the little boy. He had the look of an eighteenth century aristocrat about him. He had his mother's dark hair, although the natural curls that had been straightened without mercy in her case, had been left to flourish all over his head and crinkle right down over his eyebrows and onto his bony little shoulders. They went perfectly with his imperious manner. All he needed was a white lace collar to his shirt, a velvet jacket, knee breeches and buckled shoes to complete the illusion, but as soon as he opened his mouth, Ian winced. "I'm hungry," he whined. "Mum said you've got some chocolate biscuits. I want one."

Ian waited without success for someone to correct his bad manners. Finally, he said, "I don't know about any chocolate biscuits. We'll have to ask Pippa."

"Who's Pippa?" the child asked. "I want one *now*." His mother's grey eyes stared out from his pale face, not cold in his case, but sulky and bad-tempered.

"Bryce, you'll have to wait a minute." Tim's voice was tired and apologetic.

"Come on," Ian said, firmly. "Pippa's through here." He took hold of the boy's hand and led him through to the West Wing.

He caught Pippa's eye as he entered the room and gave her a significant frown which she understood straight away. "Pippa, meet Bryce," he said.

She stood up, her eyes taking in the little boy standing before her. She smiled. "Hello, Bryce," she said.

"Can't see any biscuits. Is that a baby? Babies are smelly."

"Well, we were all babies once, you know," Pippa said, glancing up at Ian, who raised his eyebrows at her with a, *see what I mean?* expression on his face. "I think I've got some biscuits in the kitchen. Do you want to come and have a look with me?"

"S'pose so."

"I'll take him, Pippa," Isobel said. She had heard this exchange and thought she could charm the boy out of his obnoxious attitude. "How do you do, Bryce," she said, making a grab for his hand and shaking it, gently. "I'm Isobel. Come on, let's raid Pippa's cupboards. If we're very lucky, we might even find some orange juice for you."

Millie's ears had pricked up at the word 'biscuit' and she followed them, her nose twitching. "Look, we've got company," she said. His eyes followed hers as they acknowledged Millie's presence. "I don't know about babies, but dogs can be pretty smelly sometimes. Do you like animals?"

Bryce pulled a face. "I don't like dogs," he said. "Mum says they're a nuisance." Isobel realised her challenge was not going to be an easy one.

Tim was busy introducing Jasmine to the rest of the room and then he left her to discuss the weather with Ivy and Edith, while he went over to talk to his sister. "Are you all right, Pip?" he asked as their cheeks touched.

"I'm fine. Thanks for coming. It's good to see you."

"Are you sure?"

"Yes," she said and then, noticing his doubtful expression, she added, "Well, I am most of the time. Phoebe is sweet, isn't she? Have you noticed she's got my hair? I still have a few wobbles of course, but usually about practical things. Funnily enough I've never been a Mum before, so it's quite a steep learning curve for me." She giggled. "You've been very secretive about your lady. How long have you known her?"

172

"Not long. What d'you think?"

Pippa shrugged her shoulders and turned slightly towards Jasmine. "She seems Ok. Very smart. Obviously I don't know her well enough to give you a proper opinion. If you're happy, surely that's all that matters? Why are you bothered what I think?"

Tim looked a trifle sheepish. "She could be *the* one," he said.

"Oh. I *see.*" Pippa rolled her eyes. She had heard the same story from her brother at least twice before.

"I know what you're thinking. She could be, though. I admit Bryce is a bit of a handful but I'm sure I can manage him. He hasn't had much to do with his father, you see. Mark just seems to drift in and out of their lives when it suits him. It must be unsettling for the poor little chap. I think I can make a real difference."

"Right," Pippa said, unsure of what to say next. "She seems a few years older than you."

"Only four years. That's nothing."

"No. Anyway. I'll go and ask Mum to make the tea as she's in the kitchen already. I expect she'll find it odd to have two grandchildren in quick succession." She turned to go and then backtracked. "Oh, by the way, how are you getting on with Jane?"

"All right, as it goes. She knows her way around a computer and she's had to deal with some awkward clients. Handled them well, too. Seems unflappable. Actually, I'll be sorry when Di gets back from her travels. Jane is much more interesting. Did she tell you about her gap year?"

At Migay Lodge, Susie was making progress. "Have you taken it all in now, Dad?"

"Yes I have. Thanks Susie. Was that the front door? It must be your Mum back. She'll want to read this, too, you know."

"She came home with Jane ages ago," Susie said. She was not to be so easily deflected from her purpose. "Right. Now I need you to ring Uncle Ian and tell him you want to see him. Make it some time this evening and I'll come with you."

"I don't think I can."

"Why not?"

Mike shrugged, unhappily.

"Shall I do it then? I'll say I want to see the baby and you can give me a lift and tag along. How's that?"

"I really don't know."

Susie could tell he was wavering and she was not about to give up. "Well, I do. I'm going to do it right now. All you have to do is just sit there and listen."

She had given him no option but to do as he was told. Standing in front of the door as she was, escape was impossible. She pressed buttons on her mobile and waited. "Is Uncle Ian there please? ... Hi Isobel. It's Susie ... Yes ... Thanks ... Hi Uncle Ian, how are you? ... Yes, fine. How's Pippa?... Good. I was wondering if I could come round and meet my new cousin? ... Tonight? ... Great. ... Oh is he? Well how about seven o'clock? ... Lovely. See you then. Byeee."

Susie had a glint in her eye as she flipped her mobile shut. "There you are, Dad. Tim's round there at the moment, but Uncle Ian said tonight would be fine. That was pretty painless wasn't it?"

Mike was unusually contrite. He knew it was time for a reconciliation, but he had not been able to work out how to achieve such a thing, himself. He was also grateful for his daughter's help. "Thanks, Susie. Am I allowed to see your mother now?"

"I suppose so. We'll both go. She's not going to believe this, is she? Well done, Dad. You've been very brave. Come on then," she said beckoning him towards her. "They're probably waiting with Gramps in the kitchen."

As the front door closed on their visitors, the inquest began. "What did you think of Jasmine, darling?" Isobel asked her husband.

Adrian was not prepared to be drawn. "Not sure."

Edith was more forthright. "I thought Jasmine was a bit too full of herself and Tim seemed on edge."

"That Bryce needs taking in hand," Ivy said.

Adrian nodded. "I'm inclined to agree with you, there."

"You do have to feel sorry for him, though," Pippa said. "Tim was telling me that his father's practically abandoned him."

"I wonder why?" Isobel asked.

Ian was the last one to comment. "I didn't like her eyes."

Pippa giggled. "That's a funny thing to say."

"I know what you mean," Adrian said. "Bit of a cold fish."

"You can tell a lot from someone's eyes," Edith said. "What a shame I didn't read her tealeaves."

25

Garth, as good friends do when called upon in an emergency, had spent quite some time over the previous few days trying to support Ian. They had talked long into the night on several occasions.

Chrissie had taken one of her home-made curries round to Blain Gardens because they were both concerned that he might not be eating properly. She felt relieved when he had told her the Hardale cavalry would be arriving soon. She hoped her visit and the wholesome food would help to sustain him until then. Neither of them had seen Phoebe as yet and they had decided to leave their visit until Pippa had been home from hospital for a few days and things had settled down again.

It was Mike's attitude that had given them the greatest cause for concern. Everyone knew he was a rough diamond, but where Ian was concerned he had always played the big brother card with relish. They could not imagine what had happened to have made him so unsupportive and so insensitive. Especially after the care he had taken of his brother when their mother had died and his generosity over the wedding.

Ian had told them all about the conversation at the fish pond. It was to them that he had turned for comfort after that disastrous encounter and they had picked up his shattered pieces afterwards as best they could.

They did not understand. How could Mike have dismissed Phoebe so callously and how could he not have made things right later? He must have realised that Ian was devastated and in need of a steadying hand. Neither could they understand why Gaynor had not intervened in the matter. Garth had a lot of time for Gaynor. Why had she not tried to get the brothers to talk to each other before now? Ian needed Mike, whether he would admit it at the moment, or not. Sadly, the whole situation seemed to have spiralled out of control.

Garth also wondered if there was something more he could have done to help. Had he known of Susie's intervention, therefore, he would have been the first to applaud it and to wish her success. Susie was making an attempt to paper over the cracks in their relationship. She was the bridge that could unite the two brothers and the someone who could restore that unique and symbiotic relationship that made the *Chisholm Boys* what they were.

She did not see herself in that way, of course. She just wanted everything to be as it always had been. She loved her father and her uncle and she knew they were both hurting. She was the only one who could do it. Pippa was in no state to help anyone. Mike had warned Gaynor off and he had pushed Jane away. Susie had to succeed.

And so, it was with dogged determination and a grip of iron that she propelled her father up the drive of twenty-seven Blain Gardens that Sunday evening and forced him to ring the bell.

"Come on, Dad. It's not that difficult. He's your brother. Remember?"

Ian opened the door. The 'welcome' smile faded from his face when he caught sight of his brother lurking in the shadows. "I wasn't expecting your father," he said in a voice quite unlike his own.

Susie was unfazed. "Dad's got something to tell you," she said. "Shall we do it out here or can we come inside?"

Ian suddenly remembered his manners and ushered them both into the house. He pushed the dining room door open a fraction with his foot. "Let's go in here," he said tersely and then he gave the door a good shove with his fist.

"Dad's been feeling awful," Susie began as Ian shut the door firmly behind them.

The dull thud of wood on wood resonated in Mike's head. He had visions of an interrogation suite, a naked light bulb dangling from the ceiling. Well outside his comfort zone, he was feeling horribly exposed. He had been trapped in a net of his own making, stripped of his pride and thrown into a cell of self-loathing. His daughter's voice echoed in his ears. He examined his shoes with avid interest and remained unresponsive.

As her father seemed to have been struck dumb, Susie carried on, "He's sorry he behaved the way he did and he's sorry for the things he said and he's sorry he wasn't there for you when you needed him. In fact," she said, following those two prosaic words with a dramatic pause, "He is extremely sorry about everything."

Mike, incarcerated as he was in solitary confinement, his cell door securely closed, thought he could hear water dripping from bare brick walls and rats scurrying down a nearby tunnel. But still, he said nothing.

Susie reckoned he had earned a reprieve and prompted him to speak up for himself by addressing him directly, "Aren't you Dad?"

Slowly, he raised his eyes to Ian's face. He looked pale and anxious, his discomfort obvious. His mouth felt dry and he had to swallow twice before he managed to speak. "Susie's right. I am sorry, mate. Very sorry. I was ignorant and stupid and I admit it," he said in a small voice.

Ian could feel his resolve melting. "I can understand how you didn't want it to be true Mike, but what I can't understand is how you could trivialise it like that. That hurt coming from you."

Mike hung his head and muttered another apology.

At this point, Susie was beginning to feel really sorry for her father and she decided to say something in his defence. "He couldn't hack it, Uncle Ian. He felt guilty that we were all right and Phoebe wasn't. He didn't realise that it's no big deal these days and that Phoebe will be able to lead a full life. He's read up on the condition now and he understands much better, what it's all about. Couldn't you give him another chance? Please? Just for me?" she wheedled, putting on the voice of a much younger Susie. This had the desired effect and it made Ian smile in spite of himself.

Mike noticed the smile and it gave him courage. Somewhere inside his head he heard the cell door creak open and he could feel the warmth of the sun on his face. He sounded hopeful. "That's all I want, mate," he said. "Just one more chance. I'd like to say hello to my little niece while I'm here. That's if you'll let me, of course. I'll understand if you don't want me to. I'll go straight home again." He wrung his hands while he waited for the final verdict. Susie stood beside him, her arm tucked into his.

Ian only had to think for a second and then he said quietly, "I accept your apology."

"Cool," Susie said. "Now you can both shake hands."

Ian took Mike's cold hand in his warm one. Immediately, he felt the lead weight that had been lying on his heart for the past few days, lift. "Of course you can see Phoebe. She's doing very well, I'm pleased to say."

"Thanks mate," Mike said and then, overcome with emotion, he pretended to have a coughing fit. Ian patted him gently on his back until he recovered, after which Mike tried to explain to his brother in his own words, why he had acted the way he had.

Susie left them to it. She had played her part. She thought her father could eat the remains of his humble pie in peace, without an audience. Also, she wanted to see Pippa and make the acquaintance of her brand new cousin.

Isobel and Adrian were watching some television when Susie walked through into the front room but Pippa was not in there and neither was Phoebe.

"Hello, Susie. Have you come to see the baby?" asked Isobel, getting up from her chair and walking over to where Susie was standing, just inside the door, so as not to disturb Adrian's viewing. The programme was one of his favourites; all about the coastline of Great Britain. He lifted a hand to acknowledge Susie's presence and she wriggled her fingers back at him.

"Yes, I have. I thought I'd leave Dad and Uncle Ian on their own for a bit. I expect they've got a lot to say to each other and they don't need me playing gooseberry. Where's Pippa?"

Isobel was surprised. "I didn't know your father was here," she said. "Are they talking again now?"

"Yes, thank goodness. Dad is completely idiotic sometimes, you know."

Isobel laughed. "I think you'll find that's a common characteristic in men," she said. "Pippa's gone upstairs with Phoebe. Try the nursery."

"Ok. Thanks," Susie said and she traipsed off upstairs. "Pippa, are you there?" she called as she reached the landing.

"Yes. Hi. I'm in here. Is that you, Susie?"

Susie put her head round Phoebe's bedroom door and saw Pippa sitting in a small bentwood chair, nursing her daughter. The floor was uncarpeted apart from an oblong rug in shades of white, pink and yellow, which had been strategically placed alongside the crib. Pale lemon walls met the white skirting and white floor giving a young, fresh appearance to the room. Ian had painted the old pine floorboards white at Pippa's insistence and against his better judgment. He had the grace to admit afterwards that the room looked very different, but attractive.

The old rocking horse stood in the far corner by the window. It bared its teeth at Susie in a benign grin, while Ivy's mobile moved slowly round above their heads, casting long shadows on the bare walls in the rosy glow of the pink ceramic lamp sitting on Phoebe's brand new chest of drawers. The lamp had been a gift from Isobel. She had been so taken with the delicate pastel flowers painted all around the shade and the ethereal fairies dancing around its base that she had bought it for her granddaughter as a welcome home present.

There was an open box of baby wipes in evidence and a plastic changing mat smothered in unnaturally rotund yellow ducks with bright red beaks. Susie could smell baby cream and she noticed a pile of neatly folded nappies on the floor next to two packs of disposable ones. The decision as to which method would be best for Phoebe had obviously not yet been made.

Apart from the white blind at the window, the room was unadorned because Pippa had not yet had the time to customise it. "Come in," she said. "We've nearly finished. Where's Ian?"

"Downstairs with Dad. I thought it was time those two got together so I brought him with me and made him apologise and explain himself. He was like putty in my hands," Susie said. She grinned and worked her hands together descriptively.

"Oh good. I'm sure he didn't mean to upset Ian like that but we were all feeling rather fragile at the time. There, she's ready for visitors now. Would you like to hold her?" Pippa lifted Phoebe from the reclining position and turned her to face Susie. "Phoebe, say hello to Cousin Susie."

"Hello, Phoebe. You are so-o-o cute," Susie said, cuddling the baby to her.

Phoebe screwed up her face and burped.

"Fine, you don't like cute. What about gorgeous?" Phoebe's little legs kicked out and her fingers held on to Susie's, as if her life depended on it.

"Yes, gorgeous it is. I quite like babies. I'd be happy to Phoebe-sit when I'm home for the holidays if you like."

"You'll have to fight Ivy for that privilege," Pippa said with a laugh. "This is one popular young lady."

26

"So, you've kissed and made up, have you? That's nice," Pippa said some time later as she and Ian were dealing with Phoebe's early morning feed.

"Yes, you could say that. I felt quite sorry for him after he'd explained everything. I'm glad Susie did what she did."

"It's good everything's back to normal again. Gaynor's little note was so sad. You could tell she would rather have said it all in person."

"How many cards and letters have we had?"

"Oh, hundreds," Pippa said with a giggle. "No, that's a bit of an exaggeration. At least forty, I think."

Phoebe emitted a tiny squeak and blew some bubbles across her mouth as if to indicate her approval. Ian smiled. He was relieved and thankful that his life had finally regained some sort of balance. Phoebe was slowly and surely winkling her way into everyone's hearts with each curl of her fingers and each snuffle of her little nose. He and Mike were friends again, but best of all, Pippa was much happier and finally beginning to come to terms with everything. "I think you should go with your mother, SweetP. It will do you good. Before you know it, I'll be back at work and then you'll have to do everything on your own. You won't be able to take a break."

"I might. I'm going to decide tomorrow. I'll probably feel more like it by Friday. Are you sure you'll be able to manage without me?"

"We-e-ll, it will be difficult, but I'm sure the terrible twins will help me out."

"Never let Ivy hear you call them that or she'll lynch you."

Ian laughed. "I wouldn't dare."

"They do seem to be joined at the hip, though, don't they?"

"I'm sure it's good for both of them. Mrs. E was very lonely after my Mum died."

"I remember you telling me."

"I wish Mum was here," he said, yearning clouding his eyes. "She would have loved Phoebe."

Pippa passed the baby over to him and gave him a kiss. "I don't think she's far away," she said gently, "And she's a part of Phoebe, just as you are."

Ian and Pippa weren't the only ones up and about in the early hours of the morning. Alice was pacing the floor with her son. Oliver had developed a cold and he could not sleep. As she rocked her baby and sung him a song, the words made little sense to him. His mother's soft voice was all that he needed though, plus the comfort of her loving arms around him and as he sucked his thumb, his eyelids gradually drooped and he started to snore in a gentle, baby-like fashion.

It was unsurprising that the words of the song meant nothing to him. They were variations on the theme of, *Ian and Pippa, what shall I do, oh what shall I do?* to the tune of *Money Makes the World go Around,* because Mike was not alone in feeling guilty. Alice felt dreadful.

There she was, a healthy baby in her arms and not a care in the world. The only special needs Oliver had, were the extra cuddles he needed until his cold cleared up, which she had every confidence would happen within the next few days. Pippa, on the other hand, would have to deal with Phoebe's special needs for ever.

She had sent Ian and Pippa a card of congratulations on the safe arrival of their baby of course, but she had not been to meet Phoebe. It was a nettle she had not as yet grasped, because it stung far too much. She had discussed her dilemma with Simon. He had understood her concerns but felt sure Pippa would appreciate a visit from her friend. He had even offered to look after Oliver so that they could have a good heart to heart in peace. Alice's nocturnal meanderings and their choral accompaniment had ultimately led her to the conclusion that she could not put off the visit any longer. She decided to find out if she could go and see Pippa the following afternoon.

She snuggled her sleeping son back down in his cot and tiptoed out of his room. Back in her own bed, she tucked her cold feet into her husband's warm ones. He stirred a little. "I've decided to go tomorrow," she breathed into his ear.

"What?"

"I'm going to ring Pippa in the morning and see if I can go round after lunch."

"Right." He wriggled his toes away from her unnaturally cold ones. "I'm going to buy you some bed socks," he said and promptly went back to sleep.

Isobel and Adrian had decided to take advantage of Alice's visit to go out shopping. Ian would be there to let her in if Pippa was dealing with the baby when she arrived. He still had the new baby seat to fit into his car. He had not decided on a replacement for the car but as things were beginning to calm down, he thought he could now put his mind to some serious research and finally come to a sensible decision.

Alice turned up shortly after Isobel and Adrian had gone out. "Where's Ian?" she asked after she had given her friend a big hug. "I've got six bottles of Summer Lightning here. Simon said to tell him it's to wet the baby's head. He reckons it's better than champagne any day."

Pippa giggled. "He'll like that. I'm sure you'll see him before you go. I told him I didn't need a minder, so he's gone off to fix the baby seat into his car. I'm surprised you didn't see him on your way in. Perhaps he was in the garage looking for tools or something."

She held up the three dresses Alice had brought with her as a gift for Phoebe. One pink, brushed cotton, with a round neck and several rows of smocking, its long sleeves gathered into a cuff; one a very pale lemon with small white daisies embroidered on both puffed sleeves and one mauve needle cord pinafore dress with two heart-shaped pockets attached to the skirt. "These dresses are so sweet," she said. "And chocolates? Alice, you're spoiling us."

"You deserve spoiling. All of you. Now," she said, settling herself comfortably on the sofa beside Pippa, "Tell me all about it."

Pippa did her best to satisfy her friend's curiosity and shed a few tears in the process. Remembering some parts of the last few days was hard for her. As she listened, Alice felt her own eyes moistening. "Have I told you everything?" Pippa asked. "This feels like the Spanish inquisition."

Alice laughed. "I think so."

"Good, because I've got something I want to ask you. Mum wants to take me to Marble Hall before she goes back and I can't decide whether to go with her or not."

"Is it the Marble Hall at Horsham?" Pippa nodded. "You just have to do it, Pippa. It's superb. A group of the girls from the airline used to go. They made regular dates after a stint on long haul it's so relaxing there. I tagged along on a couple of occasions. You'll love it. Really. The massages are out of this world and the food's quite special, too."

"Mmm. Sounds good but I haven't left Phoebe yet. I don't know if Ian will manage ... and I'm still breast feeding."

"Well there are ways round that. Go. I'm sure you'll enjoy it when you get there. It will do wonders for your stretch marks."

Pippa giggled. "What stretch marks?" she said. "Alice ..."

"Yes?"

"Did you feel a bit lonely after Oliver was born?"

"What d'you mean, *lonely*?"

"I miss the little chats Phoebe and I had before she was born."

"Pippa, you are seriously weird. Babies in the womb do not talk back. Although I did read somewhere that talking to yourself keeps you sane. Apparently it's supposed to lift depression and aid concentration. I must give it a go. I'm surprised your Mum didn't send you some information about it."

Pippa laughed. "Mum stopped sending me all those tips ages ago. Anyway, all I'm saying is that when I'm on my own now, I miss that feeling that there's someone else with me all the time, wherever I go. You're never alone, are you? Not until the actual birth. Of course she didn't talk back, but it didn't stop me talking to her. Didn't you have chats with Oliver before he was born?"

"I guess so, but after he was born I was just relieved to get back into my jeans again and I was too busy doing all his washing to be lonely," she said, matter of factly. "So how do you like being a mum, Pippa?"

"Mmm. Dunno. Can I reserve judgment? I haven't been in the job for very long."

"I think what I'm trying to say, is ..." Alice looked serious, "... do you find it daunting that Phoebe has Down's?"

Pippa thought for a minute. "No. Not any more. I admit I was shocked at first, but I'm getting used to it now. At the moment she's just a little baby, much like anyone else's I suppose. If I'm honest, I'm still a bit sad that she won't have the life I'd planned for her, but she is very special. She needs me to do my best for her and I'm latching on to that."

As if the baby heard this last comment, she made a little snuffling, squeaking, waking-up sort of a noise in her Moses basket and Millie, who had been lying right beside it, cocked an ear.

"Can I have a cuddle, Pippa?"

"Of course you can. She's due for a feed now anyway." Pippa picked up the baby and placed her into Alice's waiting arms.

"Oh Pippa, she's beautiful. She's got your hair and just look at her little fingers." Alice was surprised at how adorable Phoebe was and as the baby arched her back and prepared to make a polite request for her tea, she realised that she had been worrying over nothing. Pippa was fine. The baby was fine and Alice was sure Phoebe would do very well.

Alice was not Pippa's only visitor that day. Shortly after she had gone home and Pippa had fed the baby and she was just settling her down again, someone else appeared bearing gifts for Phoebe and for Pippa too. She had heard about the baby from a round robin e-mail Mike had sent out at Ian and Pippa's request immediately after the birth. She had only learned of Phoebe's disability a couple of days later, on a scheduled visit to Linchester for another reason entirely, which had conveniently coincided with her desire to find out how her old pupil was managing.

To say that Pippa was surprised to see Jacinta Scott was an understatement. She was also pleased. It meant a lot to her that Miss Scott had made a special effort to visit her and meet Phoebe. She ushered her old teacher into the West Wing where they both sat down on the wicker two-seater, a peaceful Phoebe in Pippa's arms.

Miss Scott looked around the conservatory with approval. "This is nice," she said. She glanced through the windows. "You've got a lovely back garden. Mine's ever so small, but I get a lot of birds in it. Do you see a lot of birds, here?"

"Yes we do. Mainly blue tits and blackbirds. Oh yes, and some big fat pigeons. They look so self-satisfied, don't they? Millie soon sees them off and I'm quite glad. They're always flying into the windows and giving me a shock. Doesn't seem to stun them, though."

Miss Scott laughed. "Where there's no sense, there's no feeling. Is the conservatory new?"

"Yes. We had it built soon after we were married. When I have five minutes to myself, I like to sit in here and look up at the sky. It's so relaxing."

"I don't expect that happens very often," said Miss Scott. She gave Pippa a sympathetic smile and set her large, flowery, Cath Kidston bag on the wooden floor beside her. "So, how are you finding motherhood?" she asked.

"I'm getting used to it, slowly," Pippa said.

"I know how time-consuming babies are. You won't have much left for yourself any more, so I thought a nice hot soak in the bath every now and then might do you the world of good." She pulled a large bottle of lavender bath essence out of her bag like a rabbit from a hat. "This will help you relax and sleep better when Phoebe gives you the opportunity." She passed it over to Pippa.

"How thoughtful. Thank you very much."

"I've also brought some toys with me that will stimulate her senses. I'm afraid one of them is quite noisy." Out of the same magician's hat, came a carrier bag bulging with mysterious shapes, all of which seemed to clang or jingle merrily together. "And I want you to have this selection of books, too," she said, repeating her trick one last time. "Phoebe will soon need to be read to, every single day. These books have some colourful pictures in them, which she'll love. You mustn't forget to sing to her, either. Nursery rhymes are as good as anything. That's about it. I think I've finished now. Lecture over with."

Pippa giggled her giggle and stared at the pile of gifts lined up in front of her on the glass-topped table. "Thanks, again. It seems like I'm going to have my work cut out with all of this. I'll need a long soak in a hot bath after all my hard work and so will Phoebe."

"I know it sounds a bit much, but really Pippa, the more you put into her little brain before she's five, the more she'll be able to accomplish as she grows up and the more stimulation she gets, the better she will develop. It's worth all the effort in the long run. You'll see. I've got a friend who's a special needs co-ordinator at a school in Devon and I took advice from her as to what would help Phoebe the most."

Pippa was touched. Miss Scott did not seem to feel sorry for her and she was obviously not alarmed by Phoebe's condition. She did not look at Pippa with pitying eyes like some of the staff at the hospital. She had gone to the trouble of finding out what might be most useful and she had brought good sound advice with her and some practical help, too.

"Can I have a little cuddle while I'm here? I'm used to babies. I'm an aunt three times over."

"Of course you can. She loves to be rocked. I don't know where Ian's got to. I didn't think it would take him this long to fix a baby seat in his car. You hold her and I'll get us a cup of tea." Pippa handed Phoebe over to Miss Scott's eager arms.

"That would be lovely, Pippa. I saw him on my way in. I don't think he'll be long. He was just finishing off."

"Oh. Ok then. You didn't say what brought you back to Linchester this time. Surely it wasn't just to visit me?"

"That was one of my reasons, of course," Miss Scott said and Pippa had the impression she could detect the hint of a blush on her cheeks. How could that be? She decided it must have been a trick of the light; the sun was coming in at all angles through the windows and glass roof of the West Wing. Then she remembered Ian had turned up the thermostat on the central heating system earlier on. That must be it. She dismissed the idea out of hand. What would Jacinta Scott have to blush about anyway? "I have still got friends here you know." Miss Scott walked up and down the room with Phoebe in her arms. She started to talk to her softly while skilfully managing to avoid Pippa's eyes.

"Yes. You must have. I'll go and fetch our tea."

"Just milk, no sugar thank you." The sound of a gate slamming made them both look up. Miss Scott glanced outside. "I think I can see Ian coming," she said.

Pippa joined her at her vantage point. "Yes, here he is. I expect he'll want a cuppa, too."

Ian walked in through the French windows, his eyes searching for evidence of cups and saucers. "Oh good, you haven't had your tea, yet. Sorry to have taken so long. The instructions seemed fairly simple when I read them the first time. I should have known better."

"Nice timing. I was just about to put the kettle on."

"Is that Summer Lightning over there?"

"Yes. Masquerading as champagne. Simon thought you could wet the baby's head with it."

"Sound man. I'll have a bottle now. Forget about the tea. Anyone else?"

"No thanks," Miss Scott said. "I'll stick with the tea."

"Me too," Pippa said. "You sit down, Ian, you've been working hard. You deserve a rest. I'll bring you a glass. Just chat amongst yourselves, I won't be long."

27

Pippa's next challenge was to take Phoebe to the auction rooms. She had decided to postpone her visit until she had been to Marble Hall with her mother and the Hardale contingent had gone back up north. As each day passed, her mental and physical health improved and she was sure that by the time another week had gone by, she would be ready to present Phoebe to the world outside the family and her circle of close friends, without feeling too sensitive about their reactions.

Isobel could see her daughter getting stronger and more confident in her handling of the baby and she realised that her presence was no longer required. She shared her views with Adrian. "Pippa seems to be managing a lot better now. I think we could go home soon."

"Yes. I think so, too."

"We'll have our day out together and then go home after that. I'm so glad she finally agreed to come with me. I know I'm going to feel much better when we've been. I've never had the responsibility of caring for a child with special needs of course, but I do remember how tired I was when I had Pippa. I don't know what I would have done without Mum's help. This is something special I can do for her. Set her up for her childcare marathon."

"It's hardly a race," Adrian said. He felt a little hurt at being airbrushed out of his wife's life. "I was there, too, you know. I did my best to help, but you wanted to do it all yourself. Remember?"

"It was no reflection on you, darling. I was just speaking from a mother's perspective. That's all. It's not just the physical care, though that's tiring enough. I was thinking more of the way all this might mess with her head. You know, other people's attitudes towards Phoebe."

Adrian was mollified. "Right. Well, in the same way that I tried to help, so will Ian. He'll be there for Pippa. I'm absolutely positive he'll be a great help to her. You've seen the way he handles Phoebe. He's a natural."

"I know that and you did try and help me. You did your best, darling, but things were different then. You were always being called away to important meetings at the bank." Isobel pulled a face as she said the word 'bank'.

"True. It put food on the table, though, didn't it?"

Isobel gave her husband's hand a squeeze. "Yes. It certainly did that. I don't know. I suppose it's just a *mum* thing," she said. "Watching Pippa with Phoebe these past few days, took me back."

"If I know our daughter," Adrian said, "Now she's come to terms with it herself and she's got over the shock, she's not going to take any nonsense from anyone."

Isobel laughed. "You're right. I think she gets that from me."

"You might say that. I couldn't possibly comment," he quipped.

Edith also felt the time was right to leave Ian and Pippa to themselves. She had the comfort of knowing that Ivy was only next door and Gaynor just ten minutes away, so Pippa would not be short of extra help if it was necessary. Like Adrian, she had noticed how well Ian handled the baby and she no longer had any dark forebodings.

On the Friday morning, before they left for Horsham, Pippa provided two bottles of milk for Phoebe. She

194

labelled them carefully and put them in the fridge for later. She had talked Ian through everything several times. Edith and Ivy were not due at the house until mid-morning, but until then Adrian and Ian were confident they could manage.

"You won't forget to change her before you feed her, will you Ian?"

"I won't," he replied, solemnly.

"And make sure you wind her carefully before you put her back down again," she said, letting Ian take the baby out of her arms.

"Put her back down? You don't think Mrs. E. is going to leave her lying down, do you? I expect she'll be cuddled all afternoon. Just go, Pippa. We can manage." He gave her a quick kiss on the lips before he walked her to the door, carrying a contented Phoebe over his left shoulder.

"Bye, Adrian. I'm sure you'll give Ian the benefit of all your experience, won't you darling?" Isobel said with a provocative smile as her husband brushed both her cheeks with his.

"I know more than you think I do," he said equably. "All you have to do is concentrate on the driving. We don't want you wrapping the car round a tree or something, on the way there. Stay focussed."

"Come on, Pippa," Isobel said, "We'd better go before we get any more instructions. Anyone would think I'd never driven more than five miles before."

"Right we're off then. Bye, Dad. Bye-bye, baby. Be a good girl for Daddy." Pippa kissed her little finger and put it gently on Phoebe's downy red hair as she lay in Ian's arms, her dark eyes trying to focus on the world about her.

The drive to Horsham was an easy one as the traffic was light. Mother and daughter arrived at Marble Hall in good time. They parked the car in the gravelled driveway and turned towards the house. Isobel paused for a moment to study the building and its situation. "Just look at that," she said. "For two pins I'd say that we'd walked into the set of an Agatha Christie murder mystery."

Pippa laughed. "You're right. We'd better stay alert. Poirot might be in there drinking a *tisane*."

"I hope Captain Hastings is with him," Isobel said. "I go all funny when he says, *Good Lord*."

"Mum."

Isobel laughed at her daughter's disapproval. "Nothing wrong with a bit of fantasy," she said. "This is just the place for it."

The stately grandeur of the house and its sylvan setting did seem to have a fantastical air about it. It was large and low, resting comfortably in rolling countryside and surrounded by a number of huge trees but very little else. Inside the grand oak front door which was flanked by two grey stone lions mottled with lichen their furrowed brows deep in thought, were several reception rooms and a welcoming wood-panelled hall.

Pippa's eyes were drawn to the flower arrangement someone had placed in the middle of the polished reception desk. There were palm leaves in the bulbous glass vase and exotic red and orange waxy-leaved flowers. She had the fanciful idea that a hidden eye in the middle of the flame-coloured petals would snap open at any minute and that the flower would suddenly emit a loud, squawk.

"Aren't these flowers gorgeous," Isobel said, breaking Pippa's day-dream. "I wish I'd brought my sketch-pad.

I'd love to paint them."

"Yes. I was just thinking how unusual they are. Quite exotic," Pippa said.

It was no more than a few minutes before they were welcomed by a member of staff in a crisp, white uniform, her blond hair cut short and her face devoid of any sort of make-up. She ushered them into a comfortable sitting room furnished with squashy cream leather sofas and some tactile tartan throws. "Make yourselves comfortable, ladies. I'll go and sort out some refreshments for you while you wait." She left them alone to chat to each other in front of the roaring log fire alight in the huge stone fireplace.

"I love these seats," Isobel said. She looked around the room. "This must have been a very grand house in its day. Look at the plaster moulding round the lights."

"It's rather like *Le Vignot*," Pippa said, thinking of her favourite French restaurant in Linchester. "Ah. Here come our drinks." The door opened again and another white-clad young woman, her blonde hair in a neat bun, approached them with two glasses on a tray.

"You won't have long to wait," she said as she handed out the drinks. "We're just getting the treatment room ready."

"Thank you," they said in unison. She smiled politely and left them alone again.

"What have you got, Mum?" Pippa peered at her mother's glass of fizzing cloudy liquid.

Isobel took a sip. "I'm not quite sure. A mixture of apple and pear I think. With a touch of soda perhaps?"

"I think mine has ginger in it. It's very refreshing." Pippa could feel herself winding down. "What d'you think they'll do first?"

"I haven't a clue, but I think I could do with having my facial muscles stimulated." Isobel pulled at her cheeks and then sucked them in. "One of their Japanese clay facials might work. I'm expecting to go out of here looking thirty years younger, you know." She laughed at the thought of it. "You don't need it, of course, but I'd like to give it a try."

As Isobel and Pippa sipped at their drinks and waited together in a companionable silence, another group of people was shown into the room, chatting and laughing. Pippa let her eyes drift over towards them and then they widened in surprise as she recognised one of the newcomers. She leaned towards her mother. "Mum," she whispered, "It's Judith."

"Judith who?" she whispered back, following Pippa's gaze.

"Judith Crimes."

"Goodness me. That's a name from the past. I wonder what she's been doing with herself over the last ... oh ... let me see. It must be twenty years, Pippa."

"I expect she's some high flier or other. She was head girl at the High School after all. I think she went to Cambridge."

Judith's head turned at just that second and their eyes met. "It can't be," she said out loud. She left her friends and walked straight over to Pippa's seat. "Philippa Flynn. I'd have known you anywhere. What a coincidence. I haven't seen you for ages. Not since we left school I don't think. How are you?"

"Hi, Judith. You haven't changed a bit, either." Pippa stood up and the two women embraced. "I'm Ok. I'm here with my mother. It's her treat actually. I've just had a baby."

Isobel leant forward in her chair. "Good morning, Judith," she said. "Nice to see you again."

"Hello, Mrs. Flynn and well done, you." Judith's eyes automatically veered towards Pippa's left hand.

"Yes," Pippa said. She giggled as she noticed the flight-path of Judith's eyes, "I am married. My name's Chisholm now."

Judith laughed. "I always check. In my business it's best to know as much as possible about a client. You are lucky. I'm still looking for Mr. Right. What did you have?"

"A little girl. Phoebe," Pippa said and then she took a deep breath before she added, "She's got Down's syndrome."

Judith digested this information. She was silent for a while and then just as Pippa had decided to break the awkward silence, she spoke again. "I'm sorry. Did you know about it before she was born? It must be a nightmare for you."

Pippa could feel her mother bristling. She answered quickly before Isobel had a chance to respond. "Don't be sorry, I don't see it like that. To me, she is my special baby but if I'm totally honest, it was rather a shock."

"Yes, I can understand that." Judith looked away for a moment and hesitated before she added, "I think you should meet Rose. Are you still in Linchester?"

"Yes we are. Are you? Who is Rose exactly?"

"I've been living in Little Syme for the past two years or so, but my parents are still in Linchester. Rose? Well you might call her a glimpse of the future," Judith said. "Can I ring you when I get back home? I haven't really got time to chat now. I'm here with some clients."

"Of course you can. It'll be good to catch up. If you can wait a minute I'll give you one of my cards." Pippa was intrigued. She was pondering who this Rose might be as she rifled through her bag. "Ah, here's one. This is me," she said handing the card over. "Both my phone numbers are on there. Do you have any children?" She asked, guessing that this might be an answer to the mystery.

"I'm sorry to say, I haven't, although I have accumulated a few godchildren along the way, if that counts. I must get back to the others. Nice to have seen you. I'll be in touch." With a brief smile, Judith turned on her heel and went back to join her party.

Pippa and Isobel looked at each other exchanged quizzical glances, which is all they had time to do. Another efficient-looking young lady in a white uniform, this time with her blonde hair tied back neatly in a pony-tail, had arrived to fetch them for their first session of pampering. She led the way out of the room.

Isobel held Pippa back. "I think they're cloned," she said quietly.

Pippa giggled. "Maybe we'll go home looking like that, too."

"I hope not," Isobel said, patting her chignon. "Your father would never forgive me if I went blonde."

They did not bump into Judith again and by the time they had eaten their light lunch, had been massaged from head to toe and had both been drained lymphatically to within an inch of their lives, Pippa had all but forgotten about their encounter. She was now impatient to return home and see how Ian was coping.

"I've had a great day, Mum. I'm really glad you suggested going," she said in the car on the way back.

"I've enjoyed it too, sweetie. It's not often we have a chance to spend a day together, just you and me. I feel really relaxed and my skin feels wonderful. We'll have to do it again sometime."

As it turned out the day had gone well all round and apart from Phoebe suffering a prolonged bout of hiccups, there had been no mishaps at twenty-seven Blain Gardens during their absence. Edith and Ivy had coo-ed and cuddled to their hearts content and Adrian and Ian had managed a decent walk with Millie while Phoebe had her afternoon nap in the care of her two doting nannies who had watched over her like hawks.

That evening, when Ian and Pippa were getting ready for bed, she suddenly remembered her meeting with Judith Crimes. "Do you know what happened at Marble Hall?" she said.

"Yes I do, you've told me already. Several times. You had lots of pampering and a delicious lunch." He was reclining in bed, watching Pippa brush out her hair. It was one of his favourite times of the day; when everything had gone quiet and they were alone together with the time to chat. He was almost mesmerised by her arm as it moved rhythmically up and down, trying to bring some sort of order to her unruly waves. He hated to miss this evening ritual; her hair was such a glorious colour and there was so much of it.

"No, not that, silly. What I forgot to tell you was that we bumped into someone who was at the High School with me. I hadn't set eyes on her for about twenty years."

"Strange."

"Yes," she said, putting her brush down on the dressing table and climbing into bed beside him. "She said she'd call me when she got back home because she wanted me to meet someone called, Rose. I don't expect her to ring. It was one of those empty promises people make just to be polite. I haven't got a clue who this Rose is anyway."

"Curiouser and curiouser," Ian quoted. "You never know, SweetP. She might just ring up and surprise you." He stifled a yawn. They were both trying to function on less than adequate sleep and he was tired. "Are you going to turn the light off? We need to try and get some rest before Phoebe wakes up again."

28

The days were slowly lengthening and as winter sloped off to make room for spring, life at twenty-seven Blain Gardens developed its own comfortable routine. Pippa was coping well and Phoebe was thriving. Alice and Pippa saw each other regularly. They continued to share information and took turns at allaying each other's anxieties. Pippa wanted to improve Phoebe's muscle tone and she had plans to go swimming with her. Alice had volunteered to go too because she thought it would be good for Oliver and also make the activity more fun for all of them.

Pippa had other plans for the future. She intended for Phoebe to have riding lessons as soon as she was old enough. She hoped to enrol her in a gymnastics class. Long family walks to strengthen her legs were also on the agenda. She had already started to read to her every day and she was going to make sure she had enough stimulating toys to play with. She had forgotten all about her self-pity and she was constantly searching for ways to make life better for her daughter.

Ian stayed off work for another week after Isobel and Adrian went home and the week after he went back to work, Pippa decided it was time for her to pay her visit to McFarlane & Sons.

She picked a bright morning in late February and dressed Phoebe in one of the little dresses Alice had bought her, a nice thick pair of pink tights and one of Edith's carefully knitted bonnets. She added a white cardigan with tiny pearly pink buttons and then she wrapped her daughter up in her delicate shawl. Collecting her own coat from the hall cupboard, she tucked Phoebe into her brand new stroller and set out for McFarlanes, on foot.

She had deliberately picked the week after an auction so that it was fairly quiet at the sale rooms and she surprised Beth who was discreetly munching a digestive biscuit behind her computer screen.

"Good morning," she said, assuming a broad Scottish accent. "I'd like you to value some goods for me."

Hastily, Beth stuffed the last few pieces of biscuit into her mouth and glanced up from her desk. The digestive overload had caused her cheeks to puff out like a hamster's. She gulped quickly when she saw who her visitor was, resisting the urge to smile for safety's sake. "Oh it's only you, Pippa. I nearly choked, then. I thought for a minute it was someone important." She was round her desk in next to no time and giving Pippa a friendly hug.

Pippa giggled. "That's not very nice," she said. "How come I'm not important all of a sudden?"

"You know what I mean. Let's have a look at the baby." Pippa unwrapped Phoebe and let Beth hold her. "Ahh ... isn't she sweet? What tiny fingers. She's got very long eyelashes. Does she sleep well at night?"

"No, not yet, but she's no trouble really. We get a good four hours between feeds."

"Well, I think she's wonderful. I don't know how you can bear to leave her and come back to work. When are you coming back, as a matter of interest? It's much more fun when you're here."

"Make up your mind. D'you want me back at work or not?"

"Do I? The sooner the better. Mr. McFarlane has been having a few of his blips since you've been away and no-one knows how to handle him better than you do."

"Well, you'll be pleased to hear that I'm probably coming back in a couple of weeks; part-time at first. I'm going to start gradually. James has agreed, so it won't be long now."

At that moment James appeared, looking for his morning coffee. "Pippa. Good to see you. This is a nice surprise. Come on through to my office. I'd like to meet Phoebe properly. Coffee, Beth. You, Pippa?"

"No thanks. I'll be with you in a minute."

James retraced his steps. "When you're ready, then."

"You'd better go. He's got one or two appointments this morning."

"Ok. We'll have another chat before I leave."

James was sitting in his old red calf leather chair when Pippa arrived, behind his antique partners' desk, but he got up as she entered the room. "How's it all going?" he asked, cheerfully.

"Not bad, thanks, James. We've got over all the angst now. She's such a lovely baby."

"Good. She certainly is a lovely baby. She seems very content," he said smiling down at Phoebe. "I'm glad to have this opportunity to speak to you because there was something I wanted to tell you."

As Phoebe was slumbering peacefully in her arms, Pippa relaxed back into her seat. "Is there? Work?"

"No. Not exactly. Do you remember a conversation we had shortly after you met Ian? It was about Vera Chisholm's jug and a certain photograph you had found and the Model Steam Railway Society?" He sat back down again.

"I do," Pippa said. "You mean the photograph of you and the Chisholms sharing a picnic out in the countryside somewhere?"

"That's the one. Well, Hannah reminded me that in those days, the Society did a lot of fund-raising for various charities. It was a long time ago now and I'd forgotten all about it. Vera was a leading light in getting us to raise funds for the local cottage hospital. It doesn't exist any more, but at that time it was a home for people with special needs. She organised the teas when we held open days for the residents and their families. She handled our guests with sensitivity and compassion. Nothing was too much trouble to make them feel at home."

"I never met her, you know," Pippa said.

"Didn't you? She was a kind-hearted soul. Patient and thoughtful. Shame you two never met. Anyway, there's a very good reason why Hannah remembered Vera's involvement. Her own cousin had Down's. Vera met her on a number of occasions; they even went to church together a couple of times."

"I know Vera was very involved with the church."

"Yes. A great hymn singer. Tilly loved to sing, too. That was her name, Matilda. We were very unenlightened in those days you know. We called them Mongols because of the shape of their eyes and we didn't expect them to amount to much. We didn't think in terms of special needs or even learning disabilities. We never got past the mental handicap hurdle but Vera was more understanding of their needs than most other people."

Pippa nodded and let him carry on.

"When Hannah reminded me about all of this, I remembered a conversation I had with Vera on precisely that subject. She told me that she thought people with Down's needed an extra bit of love and attention, not to be ignored and shut away. She reckoned that one of their major handicaps was the way other people saw them. Of course we know now that given the right input as children, many of them can do fairly well. They can have a social life; relationships. It's not impossible for them to get jobs these days, either. I don't know if it helps, but I felt I should tell you anyway. Hannah thought perhaps Ian would like to hear about his mother's involvement."

Pippa was touched by James's unexpected reminiscences but she did not know quite what to say. He looked uncomfortable and she decided to change the subject. "I'm sure he would. Thanks for telling me. I'll pass it on. How are things going here? You didn't have very good weather for the auction last week, did you?"

"The heaven's opened just as we started and then it poured all day," James said. "Unfortunately it wasn't a very good turnout either. Not much money in people's pockets at the moment."

"No, but the weather didn't help did it? It's no fun standing outside for hours on end with rain dripping down your neck. Next month is bound to be better."

James smiled. "I've missed your optimism," he said. "When did you say you were coming back?"

Pippa giggled. "I didn't, but don't worry, it won't be long now. Two or three weeks at most."

Eventually Pippa got up to leave and after her promised chat with Beth, she went back home mulling over what James had told her about Vera Chisholm. She knew for sure that Ian would like to hear those snippets of information. She remembered what he'd said a few nights before. Now she could tell him that his mother had been there all the time and that she would have understood.

The more Pippa learned about Vera Chisholm, the more she liked her. She found herself wishing, not for the first time, that she had actually met this intriguing mother-in-law of hers.

When Ian came home from work that night, he was armed with a huge bunch of lilies. He handed them over to Pippa, along with an affectionate kiss. "Do you remember what day it is?" he asked.

Pippa looked blank. "No. Sorry. Should I?"

"It's the anniversary of that auction where Mum's jug did the business and we went out together properly for the first time. I'm not counting our trip to hear Tim at the Drunken Duck."

"So it is," Pippa said. "Fancy you remembering that. Thanks, Ian. Actually, I've got something to tell you about your mother."

"Oh? I'll just check on Phoebe and then you can tell me."

Pippa bustled about putting the flowers in water while Ian went to check on his daughter and when he came back again she urged him into a chair. "I'm going to tell you a story. Are you sitting comfortably? Then I'll begin," she said with a smile.

"Oh good," Ian said, "I like stories."

"It all started a long, long, time ago, when Vera Chisholm was just a young woman," she began and then she embroidered a delightful tale including in it all the colourful threads James had provided for her that morning. Ian listened. It occurred to him that hearing about his mother might upset him. It did not. Instead, he found it strangely reassuring. It was as if she were there, in the room with them, telling him everything would be all right.

Eventually, Pippa came to the end of her story. "So you see, Ian, your mum's been here all along. You were right the other night when you said she would have loved Phoebe. She knew all about people with Down's. She would have been sympathetic and understood Phoebe's needs. She wouldn't have dismissed her or pitied us. She would have been there for us. Supported us all the way."

"That's a comforting thought," he said, "And a very nice story, too. I didn't know anything about all of that. I must have been too small. Thanks for telling me. I wonder if Mike remembers it? I expect Mrs. E. does. I'm surprised she hasn't said anything. I'll have to ask her. How was today? Was it strange being back at the auction rooms?"

"No," Pippa said. "It was quite pleasant, actually. Everything was much the same as usual. I think they've missed me."

"I bet they have. I expect James wanted to know when you're going back."

"You're right. He did. I said I wasn't sure yet, but we'll have to make a decision soon."

"It will be whenever you're ready, SweetP," Ian said. "Anyway, I've got something to tell you too."

"Something equally nice I hope."

"I'm not sure if 'nice' is the right word. It's definitely interesting. I hope it's good and it could be expensive. It's more of a decision I've made than a story. Although I suppose you could say there's a story involved." He grinned at her.

"What are you talking about?"

"I was chatting to one of the electricians on the site this afternoon and he was telling me about his brother, whose wife's cousin owns a garage and ..."

Pippa had sussed him out and she butted in. "Your car. It's you car. You've finally decided," she said.

He was laughing now.

"And? Come on, the suspense is killing me."

"To cut a long story short, I've done a deal. It might take a few weeks to organise and I want you to give it the once-over before I sign on the dotted line, but yes, I have made up my mind."

"You infuriating man, don't you think I've waited long enough? What's it going to be?"

"A Saab convertible."

Pippa emitted a tiny squeal. "At last," she said. "Well, thank goodness for that." And then she rewarded him with one of her infectious giggles.

29

The following afternoon Pippa was sorting through Phoebe's clothes, putting away some of the items that would no longer fit, when the telephone rang. She went to answer it, thinking it was probably Alice. They had finished a long conversation together barely five minutes earlier. "All right," she said, cheerfully. "What did you forget to tell me?"

"Is that Pippa? It's Judith here," said the unexpected voice.

Pippa was startled but she recovered quickly. "Oh. Sorry, I thought it was another friend of mine. It's nice to hear your voice again."

"I wondered if you had a spare hour or two tomorrow? I thought we could have lunch together. I mean you and Phoebe of course. How is she?"

"She's fine, thanks. That sounds like fun," Pippa said. "I could manage tomorrow, as it happens. Where shall we meet?"

"How about the Cathedral tea rooms?"

"Ok."

"Twelve o'clock alright for you?"

"Perfect."

"Look forward to it. See you tomorrow."

"We'll be there."

Pippa could not believe it. She rang Ian straight away to tell him how wrong she'd been about Judith.

"Well, there you go. I said she might surprise you."

"Yes. It's restored my faith in human nature," Pippa declared. "Now I've got to decide what Phoebe and I should wear. We need to make a good impression."

"That will probably take you the rest of the afternoon," Ian said. "Phoebe's got more clothes than you have."

It was true. Phoebe had a vast array of clothes courtesy of generous friends and family members. Choosing an outfit would not be easy, but Pippa was up to the challenge. She settled on a pink velvet romper suit with matching bootees and laid them out in Phoebe's bedroom, ready for their lunch date the following day.

They arrived at the tea rooms just before twelve. Pippa had plaited her hair neatly down her back and she was wearing black trousers and a short swing coat in cream wool. Judith was already there. She beckoned her over to the table and then watched while Pippa negotiated her way carefully across the room. She parked the stroller up by the wall right next to Judith's table and looked around the restaurant. "This is the first time I've been in here for ages. They've done it up," she said.

"It hasn't been finished long," Judith said. "It's much better now. There's more room round the tables without all the partitioning."

"Mmm. I like the patio windows." Pippa had a quick look out of the new window before she sat down. "They've put a ramp out there," she said. "I notice all that now I've got a baby in a buggy. Makes easier access than a couple of dicey stone steps. It'll be nice to sit out there again. When the weather improves, of course."

"My cousin's joining us. Do you remember her? Lucy Johnson? I expect she'll be here in a minute. How's Phoebe today?" Judith took a peek at the sleeping baby. She was well-wrapped up against the weather in her a white all-in-one quilted suit and with one of Edith's carefully knitted bonnets tied in a neat little bow under her chin. Curling erratically from underneath the picot edges, were a few wisps of her auburn hair.

"She's fine. I fed her before I came out. She should sleep long enough for us to eat lunch. I don't think I do remember your cousin. Was she at the High School?"

"Yes. Lucy's a good few years younger than us, though. She married one of the Brighouse boys. Phoebe's got your hair, Pippa."

"Yes, I know. Several people have commented on it," Pippa said with a proud smile. "I remember Richard and Will Brighouse. What are they doing, now?"

"Will, Lucy's husband, he's got a smallholding and a nice little organic vegetable business. You might have seen his vans around. *Lean Greens?*"

"Oh. That's Will is it? Yes. I have seen them. Good for him."

"Richard's a journalist up in London. He's not married. Always jetting off somewhere on a story. We don't see much of him. Phoebe looks so peaceful lying there."

"She's a good little baby really."

"Have you given up work?"

"Only for the time being. I'm going back to McFarlanes soon. Part-time to begin with. Ian and I are organising the childcare between us."

"I saw from your card that you're an auctioneer. I can't say I know a lot about the sale rooms. I've noticed McFarlanes of course. Next time I'm free, perhaps we could fix up a visit?"

"No probs. What do you do now?"

"I'm into PR on a freelance basis. I like being my own boss. It means I can pick and choose my clients." Judith stood up. "They're here," she said as she waved energetically to someone just coming in through the entrance doors.

Pippa turned to look. She saw a pretty young woman with large blue eyes coming their way. Her shiny, brown, shoulder-length hair was beautifully cut and carefully streaked with blond. She was dressed casually in jeans and a colourful knitted cardigan and she was holding the hand of a little girl. Pippa could not take her eyes off her.

The child smiled as they approached the table. "Hello Judith, how are you?" she said, clutching her life-size baby doll. She was about four years' old with fly away, brown, shoulder-length hair, cut just like her mother's. She, too, was wearing a pair of jeans and a colourful cardigan, along with a pair of smart blue glasses that did not disguise her almond-shaped, pale blue eyes nor her broad-bridged nose. All her facial features were distinctive and recognisable. The little girl had Down's.

Without waiting for a reply, she looked at Pippa and carried on speaking in a low voice and with what Pippa thought was a delightful lisp, "Hello, my name's Rose. What's your name? I've brought my baby with me."

Pippa smiled down at her. "I'm Pippa. My baby's over there in her buggy, but she's asleep at the moment."

"Pippa," Rose repeated. "Can I see your baby, please?"

"Yes, go and have a peep."

She toddled over to the buggy with an awkward gait and Pippa noticed the red lace-up ankle boots which appeared from beneath her jeans with every step she took. Rose considered its occupant. "She hasn't got a dummy. My baby's got a dummy. I haven't got one because I'm too big. What's your baby's name?"

"Phoebe," Pippa said.

"Ph – ee – bee," Rose repeated. She was savouring the syllables. "That's nice."

"Come and sit down, Rose," her mother said and then she added, "Sorry. My daughter always wants to get in first. I'm Lucy, Judith's cousin."

Pippa giggled. "I thought you must be."

"Yes, I should have introduced you two, but Rose was doing such a good job at introducing herself, I thought I'd just let her get on with it," Judith said. "Let's order our lunch. What would you like, Rose? And please don't say a marmite sandwich."

"Cheeky monkey," Rose said. She thought for a moment. "Soup."

Lucy corrected her. "Soup, please," she said.

"Yes, Mum. Soup please," Rose said.

Pippa laughed. "Good idea. I think I'll have soup, too."

Lunch went well and Pippa found Lucy easy to talk to. They all chatted about their schooldays, the Linchester they remembered from then, the shops that had since disappeared and the ones that had taken their place and, finally, children. "Was it a shock for you?" Lucy asked. "You know, finding out about Phoebe."

"Yes," Pippa admitted. "But I'm over all that, now."

"I knew in advance," Lucy said. "It doesn't help much, if that's any consolation. You still ask yourself why and you wonder if you could have avoided it; you still have to deal with everyone else's preconceived ideas about how your child will turn out. People tend to stare when you're out. I ignore them. My other children are really good with Rose and so are their friends and everyone else who really knows her. A lot of the problem is ignorance." She smiled down at her daughter. "Rose is just Rose and we love her, don't we baby?"

Rose glanced up from re-arranging her baby's clothes. "Love you, too, Mum," she said with a disarming grin and then carried on with what she was doing.

Uppermost in Pippa's mind throughout their meeting was the realisation that Lucy was acting like any other mother would with a small child. She was so cheerful; so down to earth. Nothing Rose said, or did, fazed her. She corrected her when necessary and expected her to behave, which for the most part, she did.

Pippa was impressed by how talkative she was and how she was perfectly able to sit still at the table and join in with all the banter. Her expectations for her daughter had not been great up until that moment, but having met Rose and her mother, she could now see how able Phoebe might be. There were no guarantees of course, but meeting them had given her an insight into how much was achievable. She realised it was all a question of attitudes and expectations.

"It was really kind of Judith to arrange our meeting," she said to Ian when he came in that evening. "It gave me a buzz looking at Rose and talking to her. She has to wear special shoes to stop her feet from turning in, but she didn't seem to mind. She sat at the table with us and ate her lunch without any help. She knows so much and she's only little. She won't be four until next month. I just know Phoebe is going to be the same. Lucy's lovely too. They only live a stone's throw away from the Skipper down by the canal. She's got two other children and she was telling me all about them. Anyway, we've arranged to meet up again."

"That's good, SweetP. I expect you're going to have a whole new group of friends now. Phoebe's going to have her own friends too. Before we know it, she'll be walking and talking and we'll have to think about playgroups and schools."

"Don't wish her life away," Pippa said. "I like her just the way she is at the moment; I don't want her to grow up too soon."

30

"Did you say Mike was taking you to pick up the car?" Pippa said over the breakfast table one Friday a few weeks later.

"He offered. I thought I'd take him up on it seeing as you're busy. I really need to advertise the other one."

"Doesn't anyone on the site want it?"

"No-one's said anything."

"It's a good job he offered because we don't really want to miss our swimming session," Pippa said. "We've been looking forward to it for ages, haven't we Phoebe?"

At barely eight weeks old, Phoebe was in no position to reply, but she sucked her thumb with relish and grabbed at the loose ends of her mother's hair. Pippa giggled. "See how smart she is? She knows exactly what I'm saying."

Ian grinned. "How could I doubt it? Mike was quite keen when I mentioned it to him. I was surprised. He seems to agree with everything I say at the moment. It's a bit creepy. I think he's still ashamed of the way he behaved when we found out about Phoebe. I've told him a million times to stop apologising and that we've forgiven him, but it makes no difference."

"Every cloud and all that. I don't know why you're so worried. Make the most of it. It won't last for long. Before we know it, he'll be back to his grumbling again."

"You're right. That's Mike for you. At least he's not moaning about our flexi-time arrangement." Ian looked longingly at his daughter. "I wish I didn't have to go to work at all. I'd be quite happy looking after Phoebe all day, every day."

"Well, it's my turn today. Two days at work is just about right for me at the moment."

On the three days she was at home, Pippa did everything with Phoebe. She loved their time together and made the most of it, but she also enjoyed her two days at the auction rooms when Ian took over. Phoebe was getting bigger and stronger by the day and developing her own personality. She did not seem to mind the change of carer, but she preferred the sling Ian used to carry her around rather than the stroller, which was the method of transport Pippa favoured.

Ian looked forward to the days when he had sole charge of his daughter. He enjoyed lying on the floor with her, showing her how her toys worked. He made funny animal noises to amuse her and rocked her to sleep in his arms. He took her for walks with the sling tucked underneath his coat and Millie by his side. He gazed at her when she was sleeping and soothed her with gentle words when she cried. He was always reluctant to tear himself away when it was time for work.

"Right. Well. I can't put it off any longer. It's time I wasn't here. Have a nice swim, girls. See you later." He kissed Pippa and then Phoebe and set off for the building site.

Pippa put the baby down while she tidied up the kitchen and then she packed everything they needed for their swimming session before she went to fetch her daughter.

Phoebe was lying on a blanket on the floor of the West Wing gurgling merrily to herself and kicking her legs about, surrounded by some of the toys Miss Scott had brought her. "Are you ready, Phoebe? It's time to go swimming. You're going to be mummy's little water baby." Pippa picked up the baby and cradled her in her arms, smiling tenderly at her as she did so.

Phoebe looked hard at her mother's face, the end of her tongue protruding slightly from her moist, pink, mouth. She drank in her mother's expression, her forget-me-knot blue eyes searching her mother's green ones. She was concentrating hard, her eyes almost squinting with the effort. Suddenly her face relaxed. Her lips parted. Slowly, tremulously, her mouth broke into a smile.

Pippa stared back at Phoebe, her own smile frozen to her lips. Had she just seen what she thought she had seen? She could not believe her eyes. She blinked, but it was still there. Phoebe was smiling. A real smile. Her first smile. If only Ian had not gone off to work so soon. If only he had been there to see it. She could not wait to share it with him. Her lips thawed, her smile broadened and she felt her heart warm towards her little girl, as it did quite often these days. This time, though, it was different.

This time, simultaneously, butterflies stirred in Pippa's stomach. A miracle was in the making. The mobilisation of those infant muscles had forged the last link in the unbreakable chain connecting mother with child.

In that instant, Pippa vowed that her daughter would have everything any little girl could ever want, from fairy wallpaper in her bedroom to her own playhouse in the garden and even, perhaps, her own little pony, because in that same instant, something else had happened. Something even more significant.

Her baby's first smile, such a simple and natural thing, had been all that was necessary to make her realise that the promise she had made several weeks before in a stuffy hospital room filled with flowers and the echoes of gut-wrenching tears, had ultimately been fulfilled.

She knew now with absolute certainty that she loved Phoebe. Not in an unemotional, airy fairy, politically correct fashion; the love that overwhelmed Pippa was elemental, unconditional and endless.

It did not matter that her daughter's life was going to follow a different path from the one she had expected when she was carrying her. She was unique, special, her own person. Whatever she achieved would be a bonus.

What was important was that Pippa would make sure she was happy and fulfilled but most of all, very much loved. She did not want her to be any different. Phoebe was who she was.

She cuddled her daughter to her, unwilling and unable to unpin her own smile. "Come on, my precious," she said. "We're going to ring Daddy before we go. We're going to tell him what a clever little girl you are."

Phoebe's face was solemn as she listened to her mother's words and tried to read her face. The minute Pippa stopped talking, their eyes connected, melted into each other. Phoebe's rosebud lips moved slightly and then, to Pippa's delight, she performed her miracle one more time.